In the Shadow of a Master

In the Shadow of a Master

The Unknown Chronicles, Knowledge, and Secrets of
Master Yeshua (aka Jesus Christ) and Mary Magdalene

By

Robert J. Newton, J.D., N.D.

In the Shadow of a Master

Dr. Robert J. Newton

Beyond the Bounds of Earth Publishing
Entertainment and Education | Great Motivational Talks

ISBN: 978-0-9961371-9-5

Also available on Kindle

Dr. Robert J. Newton
20253 Evening Breeze Drive
Walnut, California 91789
www.drrobertnewton.com

Dr. Robert J. Newton, J.D., N.D.,
3rd Degree Kriya Kundalini Master,
3rd Degree Ascelpiad

Ordering Information:
Quantity sales. Special discounts are available on quantity purchases by corporations, associations, and others. For details, contact the publisher at the address above.

Cover Design Artwork:
Jane Markey | Dublin, Ireland

Printed in the United States of America
First Edition: 10 9 8 7 6 5 4 3 2 1

Dedication

THIS BOOK IS DEDICATED to those who still wonder about the lost years of Jesus...

Isaiah 49:2

*He has made My
mouth like a
sharp sword,*

*In the shadow of His
hand, He has
concealed Me;*

*And He has also made
Me a select arrow,*

*He has hidden Me in
His quiver.*

In the Shadow of a Master

Dr. Robert J. Newton

Table of Contents

In the Shadow of a Master

Dr. Robert J. Newton

In the Shadow of a Master

Dr. Robert J. Newton

In the Shadow of a Master

Dr. Robert J. Newton

Acknowledgements

THANKS TO DR. ALEXANDER KOSHEVOY and Dr. Som Pol, Vedic scholar and priest—for providing me verifiable information about Jesus in India; also, Levi, who wrote *The Aquarian Gospel of Christ*; Dr. Rocco Erico and Richard Hill of the Church of Daily Living for sharing Dr. George Lamsa's *Aramaic Bible* and Dr. J.J. Hurtak's, *The Keys of Enoch—for* providing me elucidation about Jesus/Esau/Yeshua, and other salient matters.

Maybe even more important, is the feminine energy and support of my wife, Bertha Eloina Hobart Carlton Nash Newton; my deceased wife, Charlette Newton Smith; visionary artist Jane Markey, who did the special picture of Jesus for this book, teacher and author, Brenda J. Tenerelli; teacher and author, Virginia Lawson; Renaissance woman and visionary, Andrea Marshall; author and editor Anna Weber. Besides their support, they provide a counterbalance to my Halloween Scorpio energy, which is like a wild mustang...very damn hard to control! For my mission to Earth, this Halloween Scorpio energy is necessary yet always puts me on the razors edge, making it extremely easy to crash and burn, and yet also facilitates forays into the tenth dimension of heaven in "The Tree of Life" and the "Ninth Paradise" of the high angels!

Dr. Robert J. Newton 12-11-20

In the Shadow of a Master

Dr. Robert J. Newton

Prologue

MANY, PROBABLY MOST, CHRISTIANS believe everything ever written about the man, originally known as Yeshua. Also later known as Jesus Christ and Jesus of Nazareth, who has been referenced in the information contained in what is referred to as the New Testament. Most people have a generally limited knowledge of Jesus from the New Testament data. Even fewer people are aware that the New Testament may have been collated from scriptures, put together by the Roman ruling class in the second century, A.D. It is also conceivable they bent the scriptures to their liking, as a means to control the masses—the Roman underclass and slaves— as is superbly detailed in Roman Piso's book, *Piso Christ*. Piso is one of the Roman ruling class families, which go back into antiquity. In fact, by sharing this with us, the Roman Piso upset many people in the lineage from whence he came, the Family Piso.

The Roman Catholic Church claims to represent and promote Yeshua/Jesus Christ, from the first century AD, through Jesus' Disciples. Yet there is no known notation from Jesus that gives authority to a Roman Catholic Church to do so! Over time, this church held at least two conferences, the first and second Councils of Nicaea, in Turkey, where references to reincarnation in the New Testament were deleted therefrom, as well as other modifications to the New Testament. This was promoted by Turkish King Constantine's wife, who convinced him to get a Roman Catholic Pope to have the editing performed. In fact, prior to one pope actually assenting to the deletion, at least two other popes who would not go along with the queen's plan were killed.

We know between 50 and 62 A.D., that St. Paul wrote letters, also known as the Epistles, which he was inspired to share with various Christian communities. There are also scriptures, known as the Nag Hamadhi Documents, which were found in Nag Hamadhi Egypt in 1947 and discovered in two additional places in Greece. These documents are generally believed to be from the third and fourth centuries, A.D. and although most biblical scholars would vehemently disagree with me, my personal intuition tells me they actually go back to the first century, A.D.! These gospels include the Gospel of Mary Magdala (Magdalene), Gospel of Mary Salome, Gospel of Thomas, and The Gospel of Philip, among 48 other gospels.

These Gnostic scriptures reveal a kinder, gentler, and more open-minded Jesus than found in the New Testament, in a non-judgmental and non-dogmatic manner. Unfortunately, a great number of Biblical scholars and researchers have considered the Nag Hamadi, as less reliable sources about Yeshua. On the other hand, many of us consider them more accurate and insightful to teachings of him. We also find this more compassionate Jesus in The Aramaic Bible, in which Dr. George Lamsa, the Assyrian author who translated the Aramaic Peshitta (literally "straight, simple") New Testaments from Jesus' Hebrew tongue of Aramaic, into English. Dr. Lamsa's work in this Hebrew Aramaic dialect, was subsequently continued by his protégé, Dr. Rocco Erico. I had the honor of studying these things under Dr. Erico, at the Church of Daily Living in Costa Mesa, California, in the middle 1980's.

The Gnostic texts referenced above, are discussed in my book, *In Search of the Hidden Codes of God in the Mathematics of Gematria: Discovering the True Da Vinci Code.* I personally would never suggest these supplant the New Testament, but they should be added since they add immensely to the narrative of Yeshua/Jesus. Some of which are less inflected with the patriarchal bias, from two thousand years ago, when only men ruled the Earth and were considered superior to women!

There are many who claim that Yeshua/Jesus Christ is a mythical person, because there are other Masters from the ancient Egyptian times, including Osirus and his son, Horus, from Egypt— and Attis of Phrygia, Mithra, Heracles, Dionysus, Tammuz, and Adonis who share the purported birthday of Yeshua, on December 25th and because so many Masters share the same date, it obviously makes Jesus and the other Masters mythical, at best.

Can we consider a more open- minded possibility? It is well known the Druids and Wiccans, ancient English and European pantheistic practitioners, based on the cycles and knowledge of Nature, believed in fact the Winter Solstice, between December 21st and-22nd is a powerful and auspicious time, which is why the births of the above Masters are celebrated close to this date.

It has been written the Roman Catholic Church deliberately picked the December 25th date for the birth and celebration of Yeshua to minimize the importance of the existing Pagan celebrations, including Druid and Wicca Solstice festivals, which are widely celebrated in ancient Europe. In fact, we know Yeshua

In the Shadow of a Master

Dr. Robert J. Newton

(Jesus) was a Pisces under the beliefs of Greek astrology and December 25th could not be his birthdate; it would have to have been sometime between February 19th and March 20th. The actual date might be closer to March 20th, as the account of the birth of Jesus talks about shepherds, who visited Jesus in Bethlehem, in fields with their sheep...a time when new grass would be sprouting, which accounts for why they would be in their fields in the first place, finding forage for their flocks.

Although the New Testament, reveals Jesus was born in a manger in Bethlehem, there is also a Muslim story which claims Jesus was born in the desert under a Palm tree. There is still another recollection of Yeshua/Jesus coming to Earth in a Merkabah... a ball of light...from the center of our Milky Way Galaxy, revealed in a Christian Gnostic text, shared by William Henry, in *The Secrets of Sion*. Henry's information comes from an 8th century Gnostic text found in the Vatican Library, translated by Brent Landau, and revealed in his book, *Revelation of the Magi*. It is also said Jesus was from a group of people that were wise, highly evolved beings from the edge of the Milky Way Galaxy, from the race of Seth.

Although this clearly obviates Jesus being the born of the virgin Mary, it still would allow Mary and Joseph to be his adoptive parents. We also have Jesus himself in a scripture, proclaiming, in John 8:58, *Verily, verily, I say unto you, before Abraham was, I AM*, conceivably indicating Jesus was on Earth before his time as Yeshua/Jesus. This was presciently pointed out, as well, by Mary Baker Eddy, in *Science and Health with Key to the Scriptures*, who shared with us a very expanded view of Jesus in 1875 in this book.

From a wider perspective, none of this diminishes Yeshua/Jesus. It adds to the cache of who he was, although there are a great many Christians who proclaim the described virgin birth puts Jesus above all other Masters. It is pointed out in the New Testament, in Luke 2:41-52, when at the mere age of twelve, Jesus being in a temple during the celebration of the Passover, which likely would have been a synagogue, and amazing the elders...Rabbis...with his vast knowledge of scripture. This knowledge would have included the Torah, and could possibly have included the Kabbalah, which is the higher and esoteric teachings of Judaism, and includes the high angels like Michael and Metatron, at the top of the "Tree of Life."

We also recognize a period in which Jesus is not chronicled in Christian texts, called the lost years. In fact, there is this revealing book, called *The Lost Years of Jesus*, written by Elizabeth Claire Prophet, in which she uses sources outside of the New Testament, that details Jesus visiting Egypt, Greece, India, Kashmir, Tibet, and Persia, studying with Master teachers from these areas. During this same time, Jesus likewise shared his knowledge and wisdom of the Kabbalah, the 72 Names of God, with learned with the Essenes. It is well known Yeshua/Jesus studied with the Essenes in his homeland. The Essenes were known for searching deep into the Jewish traditions and texts, much beyond just the Torah.

Levi, in *The Aquarian Gospel of Jesus Christ*, relates Yeshua being at the Temple of Nazareth, and criticizing the rabbi there for having a narrowness of thought. He is further believed to have said that love is the golden cloud that binds the Ten Commandments together. This would generally be substantiated by the linguist arithmetic of English Gematria, where the SUN and LOVE share the number 54 and same properties, cross verifying and validating each other, and likewise, better amplifying and explaining each other. We know the sun emits a lot of light, oftentimes it appears golden, yet revealing a direct correspondence between light and love being amplifiers of each other.

Levi further revealed Yeshua declared the Jews have built a wall around their faith, and they see nothing on the other side of it. Further, Yeshua declared by some accounts that he the wanted to investigate faiths beyond that of Judaism. So, this sets a foundation that would have had Yeshua going out and exploring faiths from the rest of the World, as will be covered in this account of Him.

There are also ancient records discovered in Tibet by Nicolas Notovitch in 1894, which document a young man named St. Issa...believed to be Jesus, who was both a teacher and student of Buddhist priests and Hindu Brahmin priests and historians, between the ages of 13 to 29. Notovitch wrote about this in *The Unknown Life of Christ.* Swami Adhedananda was skeptical of Notovitch's claims but found corresponding information in Bengali texts he found in the northern Himalaya mountains. This same information was also confirmed by Nicolas Roerich in his research in the Himalayas. In a deeply personal conversation, I had with Hindu Priest, Dr. Som Pol, he confirmed St. Issa was in fact in India and was also known as St. Issa/Isha Masiya (Jesus the Messiah).

This is further substantiated by the Indian text, *Bhavishya Purana,* where Dr Vedavyas tells us this text mentions the future appearance of Jesus noted in 3000 B.C., a prophesy that reveals the appearance of Isha Putra (a son of God), born of an unmarried woman Kumari (Mary) Garbha Sambhava. Jesus was prophesied to visit India and the age of thirteen, and go the Himalaya Mountains, doing extensive tapas (penance), to attain spiritual mastery, guided by *rishis* and *siddhi-yogis.*

In the Shadow of a Master

Dr. Robert J. Newton

Dr. Vedavyas points out there were many spiritual and philosophical similarities between early Christianity and Hinduism. This will raise the hackles of many, I am sure.

Regardless, the book *Bhavishya Purana*, prophesies how Jesus would visit Varanasi, which has many Hindu temples, and other areas in the upper Punjab area of India, in the general area of Varanasi and also Buddhist Temples in Tibet near Mt. Kailash and in Nepal. In a *Telegu* book, Emperor Shalivahana asked Jesus who he was, and he responded he was Yusahaphat and also known as Isha Masiha (Jesus the Messiah) and the son of God, born of a virgin, and this dates to 115 C.E. So, we are getting cross validation about Jesus the Messiah in India and Tibet and Nepal from three different sources. The information referred to above, comes verses 17-32, and in particular, Chapter 19, of the *Bhavishya Purana*.

There is another account in the *Bhavishya Purana* in the 22nd text where King Shalivahana saw an auspicious man who was living on a mountain and his complexion was golden and his clothes were white. The King asked him, "Who are you sir?" The man replied, "I am Isha Putra, the Son of God," he respectfully replied, "and born of a virgin. I am the expounder of the religious principle to uplift the *mlecchas* (Barbarian invaders as opposed to native Aryans/Indians), and strictly adhere to the Absolute Truth. Hearing this the King inquired, "What are your religious principles according to your opinion?"

Jesus replied, "O king, when the destruction of the truth occurred, I, Masiya (Messiah) the prophet came to this country of degraded people where there are no rules and regulations. Finding the fearful irreligious condition of the barbarians spreading from Mleccha-Desha, I have taken to prophethood."

In the Shadow of a Master

Dr. Robert J. Newton

I must express my joy and gratitude for having this information "dropped into my lap!" I have been looking for this information for at least forty-five years, to verify the intuitional information about this I and my deceased wife, Charlette Newton Smith received, long ago! In light of all I have shared and will share, the raiment and golden aura around St. Issa/Isha Mishai/Isha Putra and the circumstances around his birth, would point to Jesus being the personage referred unto!

Now, it is also possible Yeshua/Jesus studied with the venerated Thoth, also known as Tehuti, who created the theology for the Egyptian tradition, the hieroglyphic language, and directed the building of temples and pyramids in Egypt, since they are both believed to be from the Race of Seth, located deep within a location in the Milky Way Galaxy. The amazing Thoth was also the major presence in Greece, and therein he was known as Hermes and Hermes Trismegistus, and he could have tutored the respected Greek philosophers, including Plato, Herodotus, Pericles, and Aristotle, among others. Examination reflects this lineage of Thoth, Tehuti, Hermes, Hermes Trismegistus is another personage associated with the venerated Enoch from the Torah/Old Testament.

It is discussed in The Book of Enoch, omitted from the Torah/Old Testament texts, how Arch Angel Michael, anointed Enoch and transported him to the many Dimensions of Heaven, from Earth to the fourth paradise/Dimension, ascending sequentially, to the tenth paradise/Heaven, which is where the very highest angels of the Tree of Life, reside—including Enoch, who became Arch Angel Metatron—next to Arch Angel Michael, and the angels just below them. The Ninth Paradise | Ninth Dimension is where high angels also reside, just below those of the Tree of Life, and share a linguistic arithmetic in English Gematria at 167, which reveal a paradise unknown to humans...a remarkably high Heaven...as opposed to Adam and Eve in the Garden of Eden, as well as Adam and Lilith, another iteration of the Garden of Eden.

This depth of awareness and knowledge shows us just how important Thoth, Tehuti, Hermes, Hermes Trismegistus, and Enoch/Metatron were on Earth, as Master teachers before Yeshua/Jesus. There were other places Thoth appears to have manifested himself, including in Sumer, at the confluence of the Tigris and Euphrates Rivers...450,000 years ago. Thoth is, covered assiduously in Zecharia Sitchin's eleven books, including *When Time Began* and *The Ninth Planet*, and in one of my books, *Beyond the Mists of Time: When Trees Ruled the Earth*. Each chronicle the time of an extraterrestrial civilization, referred to as Anunaki, from Nibiru or Mardock, in our solar system as extraterrestrials, living in Sumer, their Earth base. Besides Zecharia Sitchin, there are people like Orion Moya who have revealed the Anunaki may have given the Israelite's all their knowledge, including much of the Torah and The Tree of life. It should be noted that Thoth, Tehuti, Hermes, Hermes Trismegistus, and Enoch/Metatron could have been inhabiting more than one place on Earth, at the same time, which is an exalted Yogic power...the ability to bi-locate...to be in two or more places, in a functioning condition, at the same time!

It may appear I am wandering far afield, yet these different narratives come together to give us a vastly wider knowledge and perspective of Yeshua/Jesus, who was in fact a young Rabbi, as assigned when people were addressing him as Rabboni, in John 20:16, which means Master teacher and young Rabbi. For those who are Jewish or may be a Rabbi, you may be aware the Rabbi's do not study the Kabbalah until they are 40, from which begins *binah*...deep learning...and yet just by the huge amount of knowledge and wisdom and compassion Jesus dispensed, as well as the miracles he is chronicled as performing, it seems he would have had this advanced Rabbinic instruction, at a level far beyond his elder Rabbi's, since there are few, if any accounts of the elder Rabbis doing what Yeshua did with aplomb!

It is also believed by some, Yeshua/Jesus spent time in Tibet and Nepal, as was just mentioned, studying with Tibetan Buddhist Masters. Of all the religions, Buddhists spend the most time in deep and extended meditation and prayer, other than Kriya Kundalini Yogi's known as Satguru or Avatars and Hindu Brahmin priests. It is discussed in Bruce L. Cathie's book, *The Bridge to Infinity*, how even today, a group of Buddhist monks can levitate a multi-ton stone up the side of a cliff, by repeating a split tone mantra/prayer, repeatedly, which contains sacred and powerful vibrations that can change the shape and characteristics of what is termed, matter. This "matter," which at its essence, is only energy; no dense matter has even been detected in the Hadron super collider in twenty years or so of research and testing! The split tone comes from relaxing the voice, getting into the base range of notes, and eliciting more than one tone at the same time, at which Buddhist monks are Masters!

We know there was a person known as St. Issa in Tibet, Nepal, and India, who is believed by people in these areas as one and the same as Jesus, mentioned previously. We further know Yeshua/Jesus arranged for his disciple, Doubting Thomas, to go to India as a carpenter and to teach in India, after his so-called resurrection, which we find in the gospel, The Acts of Thomas, a Gnostic text not included in the New Testament.

In the Shadow of a Master

Dr. Robert J. Newton

We also know the three Wisemen (Magi), came from the Orient to honor the birth of Yeshua/Jesus. We find further that Yeshua/Jesus was assignated as St. Issa in Moslem texts, as well as those discovered in Tibet, Nepal, and India. This information is shared in the book and movie, *The Life of St. Issa, The Best of the Sons of Man*. Digging deeper, we find comparable information about Yeshua/Jesus and the Hindu and Yogic traditions of India, especially revealed in the miracles he performed!

We are made aware that the Kriya Kundalini Yoga lineage goes back thousands of years, if not much more, in the millions and billions range, as is chronicled as the timeline in India in *The True History and Religion of India*, by Swami Saraswathi, where he back counts the Indian long cycles of time, known as Yugs or Yugas, revealing a 1.9-billion-year timeline. There have been many Kriya Kundalini Yoga Masters who have attained immortality in their existing bodies, arriving in a state of Soruba Samadhi, which is achieved by Mastering structured meditations, call Kriya Dhyana or Dharana and extended breathing meditations of Kriya Kundalini Pranayam(a). This process is described in *The Yoga Sutras*, by Satguru Patanjali and in *The Death of Death*, by Satguru Babaji Nagaraj. *In Science and Health with Key to the Scripture*, Mary Baker Eddy boldly proclaims that Jesus never died. Although Mrs. Eddy was not aware of the following: *if Yeshua existed in a state of Soruba Samadhi, it would have been impossible for him to have died on the cross, and bled to death, because he was already in a state of immortality, in a state of super-suspension, beyond the need for breath, a heart, blood circulation and food or water.*

Sufi Master, Younus AlGohar has also postured that blood never dripped or escaped from the body of Jesus, during the crucifixion, and this was an embellishment by sources trying to emphasize Jesus' suffering on the cross! The loss of blood and pain and suffering recorded in New Testament scriptures could well have been scriptural editing, to make readers feel guilty and resigned to be sinners, certainly an effective control mechanism that could be used by the Roman Catholic Church to make people compliant and docile to the agenda of controlling the population at large!

In others of my books, *The Immortality Prophesy, In Search of the Body Immortal*, and in *A Map to Healing and Your Essential Divinity Through Theta Consciousness*, I discuss a connection between the blood circulating in a human body and how it transports the life force of God, throughout our bodies, which is known as Prana or Chi. Yet beyond this, in Soruba Samadhi, during which one achieves highly elevated states of consciousness and joins all aspects of being, including physical, spiritual, mental, and emotional. In this state, a body exists without breath, heartbeat, and blood circulation, because the body is supported via Yagna (fire), Agna (light) and Aum (the vibration and sound of creation), known as the Intelligent Cosmic Vibration, as revealed on page 369 in the *Bhagavad Gita*, in the Paramahansa Yogananda translation of this text. The Yagna and Agna discussed therein, is akin to Prana/Chi— an electromagnetic energy and force, directly associated with atoms—which are electromagnetic, and irretrievably connected to and created by our Creator/God.

Jesus knew this as well as anyone who came to Earth. He was a willing sponge for knowledge and new abilities. A lost gospel dating back to 570 A.D, although written in code, could indicate Mary Magdalene, far from being a prostitute, was Jesus' wife and co-messiah. I have some doubt about Mary Magdalene being Jesus' wife but know she was the closest disciple to Jesus as per the Gnostic Gospel of Philip...and may well have been his consort, and wife. Although *the DaVinci Code* and *Holy Blood, Holy Grail*, indicate Jesus had children, there is not incontrovertible evidence of this. When Mary Salome, Mary Magdalene's best friend, asked Jesus how she could attain Heaven, he responded that one must live a virtuous life and be barren. Being barren means without child and I have little doubt Mary Magdalene would have learned about this from her friend, Mary Salome. The Gospel of Philip also tells us the Apostle John was jealous of Mary Magdalene because the other Disciples would always go to her and ask for their questions to be relayed to Jesus, for him to answer for them.

I would also add another perspective—that of Jesus having a wife. Another son of God, Rama, an incarnation of Lord Vishnu, had a wife, known as Sita, which is revealed in the Indian classic text, *The Ramayana*, going back 330,000 years ago. Still another son of God, Krishna, another incarnation of the Lord Vishnu, had 12,000 wives, most of whom he liberated from bondage and sexual slavery.

With that, the story I am about to reveal I hope is as fascinating for you as is the writing thereof for me, as I collated things I have been learning and archiving since 1951. For your highest enjoyment and elucidation, this story will require you to be flexible, which will allow you to expand beyond your present understanding of Yeshua/Jesus. I have been carrying around this story in my head for many decades—during which time as I experienced many things about Yeshua during meditations, dreams, lucid daydreams, trances, and constant research. I am now ready to download it therefrom, with massive amounts of inspiration from our Creator/God, the Arch Angel Metatron, Arch Angel Michael, Satguru

Babaji Nagaraj, and high angel, Charlette Ann Newton Smith, as well as other angels and guiding lights!

I have been told by one of my mentors and teachers and several different psychics and astrologers, that I was with Jesus during his stint on Earth. This, of course is not possible to prove, and I will be relying on my documented powers of remote viewing to achieve my daunting task to share this story. Remote viewing has gained credence and usage, via the government agency, DARPA, where people who work for the government go back and forward in time to retrieve information stored in the energy of the atomic field on Earth and the entire Universe, which acts like a cosmic computer. This remote viewing could be compared to the Akashic records in the Indian Vedas, meaning knowledge from the skies, and comparable with celestial hearing, discussed in *The Yoga Sutras* by Satguru, Patanjali. In *the Keys of Enoch*, Dr. J.J. Hurtak discusses a cosmic computer, wherein is stored all the information and events that have transpired in the Universe, making this akin to the Akashic Records.

I am mindful that many Christians feel their religion is diluted when it is mentioned with any others. I know what I have shared and will share with you will provide evidence to the contrary…that it reinforces Christianity and indicates it wide reach far beyond what is known or accepted! At this time of immeasurable evil in the political and business class and rampant pedophilia… worldwide…we cannot afford to shun others who are devoted to God, albeit in a different way than we do!

Hey Zayin Yod, the 9th Name of God, meaning invoking angels, and Aleph Kaf Aleph, restoring things to their perfect state.

Robert J. Newton

In the Shadow of a Master

Dr. Robert J. Newton

Robert J. Newton, J.D., N.D., 3rd level Asclepiad, 3rd level Kriya Kundalini Yogi, Biblical and Vedic scholar.

Let us begin our journey supreme!

In the Shadow of a Master

Dr. Robert J. Newton

In the Shadow of a Master

In the Shadow of a Master

Dr. Robert J. Newton

CHAPTER 1

A GREAT SON OF GOD, ANONYMOUS IN THE MIDDLE OF A DESERT.

"I, JAMES, REMEMBER FIRST seeing Jesus in the temple in Judea, during our Holy Passover, when we were twelve years old, or so it appeared. He had created quite a ruckus since the elders...Rabbis...were drawn to him, partly because of the light that literally surrounded and enveloped his body, but just as much for the answers he provided to their questions.

The Rabbis looked at each other, all of them stunned and amazed. How could a mere child provide them with answers or understanding to things they could not muster? Mumbling amongst themselves, they tried to understand how a youngster was so wise and insightful. The questions...so many questions. "How does this boy know these things? Is he the promised Messiah of the Jewish people?"

In the Shadow of a Master

Dr. Robert J. Newton

Consider this in contrast to how Yeshua would be viewed, later in his life, when he began his mission to enlighten the masses in Palestine. At the Sea of Galilee and the Dead Sea, among other places, he ran afoul of the Pharisees, who were the defenders the scriptures in the Torah/Old Testament of The Bible. Although I was a contemporary of Yeshua, I was not in his inner circle at this time, but soon would become so. Although the Rabbis never taught us anything specific about the Kabbalah in the synagogues, we were told it was the higher teachings of Judaism, which could only be understood and perused by the older Rabbis. We were told only the Rabbis age 40 or older were allowed to study the Kabbalistic texts and "The Tree of Life," which we also knew as *binah*...deep learning

Being the son of a farmer, who grew olives and wheat, I was quite intrigued by this "Tree of Life," but never expected to be able to learn the essence and inner secrets contained therein.

My father required me to study the Torah, the text of the Jewish masses. However, for me, although the stories of Moses and Abraham and Joseph and Shadrack, Meshack, and Abednego and Daniel in the Lion's den were interesting, I thirsted for more! I got to where I lost any interest in studying only the Torah.

Then by a providence of sorts, at the age of thirteen, right after my Bar Mitzvah, I was invited to attend a temple of the Essenes, Jewish ascetics, who lived near the Dead Sea. First, however, I had to pass three extensive examinations regarding the Torah. The Essenes knew the Torah better than any of the Rabbis because they were obsessed and devoted to it. This group were also obsessed with living pious lives, devoted exclusively to God. They avoided sin and fervently believed humans were immortal, in their origin, which was not just talked about or even considered by the rabbis or others among us. They were dedicated to the coming messiah, unlike the Rabbi's, Sadducees, and Pharisees. Little did they know The Messiah was already in their midst! With the Essenes, I got to personally meet and study with Jesus, also known as Esau and later as Yeshua, who was recruited to this temple, as well. Neither the other boys there, nor I were even remotely in Yeshua's league but we were benefited by being around his insightful genius and wisdom far beyond his years. Some of us were later to become his Disciples, described in the New Testament and the Gnostic Texts.

While at the Temple of Judea I observed how the elders/Rabbis, the Essenes were in awe of Yeshua's knowledge beyond that of their own traditions and texts. Jesus, seemed to me, to be preparing for a teaching mission for the masses in the future. Hence, he taught his contemporaries—us—about the true spiritual nature of ourselves as divine beings directly from our Creator-God. We were beings of energy and light...and not as the sinners we were told we were from the Torah. He assured us, sinners were not bad or condemned people, but rather without knowledge; simply not knowing better...ignorant of our divine origins; that sin itself, simply denoted ignorance.

The Essenes and Yeshua often referred to the 7th Name of God in the Torah, Aleph Kaf Aleph, which also intimated we were perfectly created, divine beings. We found this also revealed in Exodus 14:19-21, as Yeshua revealed to us. This 7th Name of God was part of the spiritual teaching, which until this time were missing in my life. I remember thanking my Essene teachers and Yeshua for sharing this with me, as it confirmed my long-held hunches about a perfect creation of the The Creator, no one else was even considering...let alone, teaching!

5

Yeshua just wryly smiled at me and responded mentally/telepathically, *you deserve to know this higher Jewish knowledge, and I can tell you have been searching for it from an incredibly young age. I can see we are of one mind and this is just the beginning of our relationship. Rejoice, James, for the force and spirit of the Lord runs deep in your veins!*

I was completely overwhelmed with joy but felt unworthy of Yeshua's praise, but I joyfully responded, "Hallelujah, Rabboni! I am blessed beyond any and all measure to have met and associate with you! Kadoish, Kadoish, Kadoish, Adonai, Tsebayoth," I continued in Aramaic Hebrew, which means, Holy, Holy, Holy is the Lord of Hosts.

Yeshua replied in a state of bemusement, "You know much and possibly you know that Lord God of Hosts is equivalent in the linguistic arithmetic of Gematria in Hebrew, at 722, means, the Strength of God, Chosen Messenger, and End of Suffering. Are not the people of Israel searching for such and in need of this?"

"I have to admit, Rabboni—I must be honest with you—I understood that having God as my host, was a boon to me and us, but I did not know of these deeper meanings and permutations you mentioned, contained in Gematria, but I am so glad to have these deeper insights you have shared. It is making things click... they are fitting together with a meaning not available in any other way or source!"

Yeshua just looked over at me, with a customary wry smile to which I had grown accustomed, and gently nodded his head up and down.

Yeshua and I and the other male students at the Essene Center, studied and pondered the 72 Names of God from Exodus.

We also were later introduced to the 72 Angels of God, which cross referenced each other— and with the 72 + 72, we had the holy number of 144, which total 9, signifying a complete idea or cycle. Yeshua pointed out to me how the 7th Angel of God, Anchaiah, was equivalent with the 7th Name of God, Aleph Kaf Aleph—restoring things to their perfect state—and how this angel was associated with knowledge and learning.

Yeshua directed his glance my way and said, "You and I will be going on a deep search of knowledge and learning, to foreign lands. Just you see, James!"

In the Shadow of a Master

Dr. Robert J. Newton

CHAPTER 2

A ROLLING STONE GATHERS NO MOSS.

IT WOULD TAKE ME little time to realize just how very prescient Yeshua was in what he proclaimed. At the age of thirteen, late in the year, Yeshua and I got permission from our parents to search for more knowledge around the world. We both knew we our lives would be enriched by searching the World for more spiritual knowledge and insights. We had already experienced our Bar Mitzvah ceremonies and were considered young men; as was our custom, many of our contemporaries were already married after their Bar Mitzvah's at just thirteen years of age. Yeshua had other ideas and enlisted me to go on what would become a life changing journey to many distant countries with spiritual teachers, from myriad traditions other than Judaism.

My parents had many reservations about this proposed journey; they wanted me to take a wife, from which they would receive a dowry from the wife's parents. Yet, Yeshua had a very compelling aura about him. He exuded the energy of someone who could be trusted, and he somehow convinced my parents and his parents, Joseph, and Mary, we would learn many things from other traditions that would aid us in our later lives.

Considering the tightness among Jews in protecting their religion, to the exclusion of all others, it was a major miracle Yeshua was able to convince our respective parents to allow us to proceed with our major sojourn. A sojourn, certainly, however, would be the beginning of a long stream of magical experiences—of miracles to come—at the side of Master Yeshua!

Yeshua decided we should visit Egypt first, since he was enamored with the miracles Moses performed when he was there. He told me, "There is much to learn in Egypt from the very priests there who instructed Moses in the miracles of the temple priests."

I listened raptly, eager to learn all he had to impart, and was fascinated by his next statement. "Also, when I was dreaming, I was shown a man—actually the face of a priest of Egypt—a man of great learning and wisdom, whose spiritual insights and knowledge lead the entire land of Egypt. He appeared to me as one named Thoth. I went to the synagogue and there found a text that referred to him and how he was revered throughout the land of Egypt. I wondered if he might have been instrumental in the large pyramids and temples that were constructed there."

I thought, *we need to meet him.* I conjectured, with great reverence, "We can learn from him, under his tutelage! Oh! But you must know, Master Yeshua, I would never question your decisions, since you taught me so much in the Temple of the Essene's. I know you are the Messiah our people have been waiting for. We must prepare you for your task ahead!"

"What task would that be, James," Yeshua laughingly replied.

In the Shadow of a Master

Dr. Robert J. Newton

"You know so very well what I am referring to, Yeshua. Don't pull my leg...I like them both to be of equal lengths."

Yeshua just raised his eyebrows, with a sanguine look on his face, and turned his eyes upward to the Heavens. And with little direction Yeshua then exclaimed, "Why don't you go and see if we can borrow a donkey for what will be an arduous journey, James!"

I agreed to the request and with that as my mission, spent some time looking for a donkey to borrow. Unfortunately, the only one I could find, was one with three legs. So, I waited to tell Yeshua about this until the next day, thinking he might be annoyed with me for my less than stellar effort.

I brought the donkey to Yeshua to inspect, thinking he would berate me, yet just the opposite happened.

"A three-legged donkey will work quite well for us, James...you did good!" Yeshua's enthusiasm was not overlooked by me and made me consider what might be ahead for us.

"Yes," I replied, "but it only has three legs but at least it is free, and we might have to carry the donkey, at times, Rabboni!"

"Not for long," Yeshua responded with great confidence. "Take a look at the donkey now, James...I don't think we will have to worrying about carrying it!"

To my astonishment, our three-legged donkey now had four legs. In an incredulous tone I queried, "How did you do that Master?"

"Remember the 7th Name of God, Aleph Kaf Aleph... restoring things to their perfect state? That is what I did through God, with the donkey—restored it to its perfect condition. I also used another of those names, Hey Resh Chet...connected to the light, and took that

11

light of our Father that is in Heaven and focused my attention and intent where the missing leg was, that is now no longer missing, and it re-manifested itself. I say that because the leg was always there, it just became unmanifested. The spirit...the energy of that leg, was always there, I just let our Father-Mother-God bring the donkey back to its perfect form. Don't tell anyone about this; it is just between you and me for the time being, ha-ha! For sure, now that donkey will serve us well, as he is rejoicing in his good fortune. He will bestow upon us his high adulation and be devoted to us, in appreciation of his good fortune!"

All this was really mind shattering for me, yet I knew it was just the beginning of many healing works and miracles from Yeshua. I held the greatest confidence that he was the Messiah of the Jews, and he would—at the right time—change the world much for the better!

"Get some sleep tonight, James...we are leaving early in the morning. I do not want anyone to see how our donkey has changed," Yeshua declared, as he winked at me. "Pack as much water, wine, and dates as you can and we will bring two lamb's wool bed rolls, that our trusty donkey will carry for us."

"Good night, Master," I responded. "I hope you get a good sleep too!"

"Don't worry about me James...I will be meditating all night and communing with God," Yeshua confidently asserted.

CHAPTER 3

ONWARD TO THE MAGICAL LAND OF EGYPT WITH A NEWLY REFURBISHED DONKEY.

YESHUA CAME TO MY house well before sunrise, awakened me and declared, "We need to leave Judea and proceed to the Sinai Peninsula! Is the donkey packed with our water, food, and our belongings, James?"

"Yes, Master," I replied in earnest, "we are ready to proceed on our journey!"

"Thank you, James, "Yeshua responded in a grateful tone and manner, "but you do not have to call me Master, as you have been doing…I am only Yeshua. You know that."

"Yes, I know all that, Yeshua, but I call you Master and Rabboni because of your knowledge, works, and the love you so bounteously bestow upon me and humanity."

In the Shadow of a Master

Dr. Robert J. Newton

"Have it your way, James. Just know I will always want you as my confidant, whether you call me Master or not!" Yeshua had just shared a uniquely honest feeling with me...with a compassion that warmed my soul. He just knew so well how to make people feel good about themselves, in deference to himself.

As I was still pondering the miracle of the no longer missing donkey leg, Yeshua declared, "We have about 600 mil (approx. 1500 kilometers or about 1400 miles) until we reach Suez in the Sinai so hopefully, we can do that in ten or fourteen days. We can probably stay in a manger in Sinai...relive my humble beginnings...yes?

"A Master who is a comedian...what a combination," I wryly replied.

"Thank you for noticing," Yeshua declared, "but for your elucidation we might be bending time on our journey, which will allow us to travel at the speed of light!"

"Where did you get that idea, Yeshua," I asked in astonishment.

"Remember the 59th Name of God, Hey Resh Chet...connected to the light?" Yeshua then declared in a confident manner, "the secret to moving or traveling at the speed of light is in immersing oneself, completely, therein, and merging with this allows us to travel and be propelled long distances in a very short period of time!"

"Let's concentrate on this, seeing our donkey moving with us, and see what happens because I would rather be learning from the Masters of other cultures rather than spending my time walking from city to city, unless there is a benefit for us doing that."

And that is exactly what we did, much to my chagrin, moving at the speed of light, we did indeed, and within a few seconds we

14

wound up in Suez, Egypt. As I looked over at Jesus and our donkey, I sarcastically shared with Yeshua, "You've been holding out on me my Master! You are like a magician...Magi. If your parents could see what you just did, they would be in a state of disbelief!"

"Exactly James, which is why I never did this in Judea. However, my connection to God led me to know we could do this, and you were an integral part of our light travel, as well," Yeshua declared in a matter-of-fact manner. "Let's see what is happening in Suez! Our ancestors traveled through this area as they left Egypt when they fled the slavery of the Pharaoh Ramses."

"Things were probably more exciting then, than now, Master, "I declared after surveying the town of Suez and the Gulf of Suez. "Probably the best thing we could find here is some great seafood. Unfortunately, we have no money so..."

"Don't fret, James," Yeshua declared with supreme confidence, "I will rustle up some fish for us."

Almost immediately after his declaration, Yeshua in fact manifested out of thin air two white fish that would serve as food for us.

Imagine my astonishment as I declared, "Holy God, Master, you are full of useful surprises!"

"Since you were crazy enough to come on the adventure with me, the least I can do is feed my companion, James, "Yeshua replied with a twinkle in his eyes.

"Fair enough, Rabboni," I responded, gratefully, "I will find some scraps of wood and cook our fish, which we can supplement with dates. In a few minutes I will have a fire going and when we get some coals, I'll cook the fish on some branches of desert plants"

The smell of the fish cooking made me hungrier by the minute, but Yeshua seemed oblivious to such, as he was in a state of deep meditation. When the food was ready, I used my mind through telepathy to signify to Yeshua the food was ready. Through his great psychic powers, the Master had already sensed such, but thanked me, anyway.

After we consumed the fish and some dates and wine, I began to feel very relaxed. There were small waves lapping upon the shores of the Suez Peninsula, and the negative ions from these waves made me begin to feel happy, satisfied, and sleepy. I unrolled my lamb's wool blankets, one underneath me and one on top, and began to drift off to sleep in the starry desert night. Yeshua, however, was in a very deep meditation; he appeared to me to be in deep communion with our Creator-God.

CHAPTER 4

LEAVING SUEZ FOR THE WONDER OF HELIOPOLIS, CAIRO, GIZA, AND THEBES.

IN THE MORNING, WHEN I awoke, Yeshua was again deep in meditation. As he sensed my awakened state, he smiled and spoke to me, "Today we are off to Heliopolis, and later, Cairo and Giza, Egypt, which is about 50 miles away (127 kilometers/approximately 75 miles away), so since we are passing through mostly barren desert, let's light travel again, with our donkey in tow. I am glad to see you found some hay in Suez, as feed for our donkey, James. You and I can feast on dates before we depart!"

"That sounds good to me, Rabboni, and I am looking forward to visiting the pyramids in Giza," I declared. I imagined Yeshua found it easy to read my anticipation in the tone of my voice.

"OK James, I think we will light travel directly to the city of Heliopolis and then we will make the short trip to Cairo and Giza, by donkey, soaking in the city of Cairo. What do you think of spending our time around and inside of the Great Pyramid and its two companion pyramids?"

After we ate, Yeshua manifested a ball of light, known in the Kabbalah as a Merkabah, and we were transported within a few seconds—in that ball of energy—to the city of Heliopolis, and the temple thereby, with our donkey in tow, so to speak. When we arrived at the Temple of Heliopolis, he presented himself to the priests therein.

The many priests there took a liking to Yeshua and began to pepper him with numerous questions about God, which he answered fully. Needless to say, they were impressed by his responses, including some of which he learned in the synagogue as a young Rabbi (Rabboni), and also in the temple of the Essenes. They blessed him with their words and prayers and suggested Yeshua continue to his next destination to the city of Giza, Egypt and that he connect with Thoth while there.

Yeshua thanked the priests for their audience and their insights and proceeded with me, as we used our donkey to transport ourselves to Giza, where we stayed the night under the stars in the desert, finding comfort in our lamb's wool blankets.

In the morning, after another breakfast of dates, Yeshua and I—and our donkey—embarked on our journey to the Great Pyramid. This lap of the journey found us walking since our donkey was overly saddled with our food, wine, and water. Viewing the Great Pyramid, as it intruded into the sky, was an impressive scene for me to behold...grander than anything in the entire land of Israel. Also, we could see the Sphinx, which was close by, not far away from the pyramid complex and protruding into the sky. Yeshua used his intuition and highly developed abilities of remote viewing to search for an entryway into the Great Pyramid, which was not apparent on its exterior.

"Since it is hidden by a forcefield of energy, follow me up these huge blocks of the pyramid and we will find our entrance into the pyramid, James. I had but to remember the three-legged donkey experience to understand the basis for Yeshua's seemingly supreme confidence.

"I don't see anything, Master, other than these massive blocks of stone?" I declared in a frustrated tone.

"That is because you are using your eyes, James, whereas I am my inner sight, related to my pineal gland," Yeshua noted in an instructive tone of voice, "If you let your eyes go out of focus, you might see toward where I am heading!"

I decided to follow the behest of Yeshua, all the while uncertain what I might or might not see. "Wow, you are only too right, Master," I declared with glee, thinking *there must be few only a select few who are able to see this and to enter this massive pyramid.*

"Wait until we get inside and visit the King's Chamber of this pyramid, James...it will take us to the land of the beyond." The supreme confidence, which manifested in the determined set on Yeshua's face was not lost on me.

As we entered the entrance to the pyramid, hidden from public view, Yeshua took a four-inch quartz crystal from his robe like garment and squeezed it. It emitted a light, which guided our way to the Kings Chamber, a narrow passageway of several hundred feet...in current Earth measurements.

In the Shadow of a Master

Dr. Robert J. Newton

When we arrived at and entered the Kings Chamber, Yeshua declared in a somewhat authoritative manner, "I have another quartz crystal in my robe. I will squeeze it so we can have two sources of light. Please, notice, the walls of this chamber are quarried from rose granite. It contains an ever-present energy— piezo electricity. This energy specifically is a feminine love energy, and in this chamber, it will open even the hardest heart."

"Notice James, that the angle of this pyramid is measured at 51.52 degrees, and that pyramid angle also resonates with our hearts. Of further significance, the rectangular box in this chamber, a little bigger than the size of an adult man, is also constructed from rose granite, which is called the sarcophagus. It is believed King Cheops was buried here, but really, this is an initiation chamber. I want you to get inside the chamber and lay down and begin to meditate. Breathe into your lungs, with your mouth closed and exhale in the same manner, with your mouth shut...with the breath going into your solar plexus, just above your stomach."

"I'll follow your instructions, Master, since I am sure there will be great benefit in my doing so," I humbly responded.

As I began an extended breathing meditation, as per Yeshua's direction, I felt my heart opening and I felt an intense energy entering my body—with such an intensity my face became so hot, I thought I was being consumed in flames.

I felt as if I was being pulled out of my body, into a higher state of consciousness, bathed in a field of love, and my consciousness went flying into space, until I arrived at a planet of beings who all shone as light. I felt wonderfully comfortable when I arrived, and knew I was visiting a place of which I was remarkably familiar. The light beings smiled at me and told me it was time for me to return,

20

and they would be meeting me another time in the future. I allowed my intuition...my inner guidance as such...to lead me back to my body in the sarcophagus.

When my consciousness came back to the sarcophagus, Yeshua told me that all the while I was absent from my body, there was a blissful smile on my face. When I re-entered my body, my only regret was that I had come back from the distant planet I visited, and I was surprised to see Yeshua talking to a man who had an intense aura of light around him; a man who exuded an air of great knowledge and wisdom.

Yeshua then turned and asked me, "How was your meditation...your trip to the distant planet?

"I was very pleasantly surprised, Master! I know that what I experienced has changed my perspective and understanding of things. I felt that Divine Love you have often referred to and know that experience is something that gives me a greater understanding and appreciation for our Lord God"

With a reverence in my voice, I had shared my feelings, to which Yeshua responded, "That was what I hoped you would experience, James." I carefully watched his face, and saw a certain satisfaction, punctuated with a wry smile. "I want you to meet Thoth, the Supreme Hierophant of Egypt, who created the hieroglyphic language of Egypt. He also wrote *The Book of the Dead*, also known as *The Papyrus of Ani*, which speaks of life and death and the path to immortality, which I have discussed with you, James. He is going to guide me in a meditation in the sarcophagus...the Djed...which he also discovered and conceived, in conjunction with our Lord God."

In the Shadow of a Master

Dr. Robert J. Newton

I found it difficult to contain my eagerness as Thoth began to guide Yeshua in a meditation only known by the high priests of Egypt. Performed with the mouth closed, it is an exercise that used only nostril breathing—with a deep breath into the diaphragm and then pulled up into the chest. The exhale is performed again with the mouth closed. The tongue is placed in the soft palate of the mouth, and this allows the exhaled breath to be twice as long as the inhale. Performing this secret meditation, Thoth and I watched as Yeshua disappeared into a ball of light...a Merkabah. Sometime later, out of nowhere, so to speak, we then saw Yeshua reappear—in the sarcophagus of the Great Pyramid.

After a few minutes passed, caught in the spectacle and miracle I had just seen, I asked Yeshua, "Master, I know you traveled somewhere! Where did you go?"

He gently responded to me, looking refreshed and energized as his body glowed more intensely than its normal auric field, "I went back to my origins in the center of the Milky Way Galaxy, to the Race and Planet of Seth, to meet again with my teachers and mentors there, akin to the high angels on the Tree of Life, in our tradition of the Kabbalah!"

I saw Thoth smile, sublimely, and nod his head up and down, "I sense you enjoyed your trip, immensely, Yeshua. Right?"

Yeshua answered him with a wide smile as he mimicked Thoth's head nodding up and down. After some time passed, he replied, "Thank you so much for allowing me to borrow the sarcophagus, allowing me to have a short vacation! I learned we are both from the Race of Seth. We both come from an exalted place, with highly evolved souls. It is as we are soul brothers! Can we please ascend now to the Queen's Chamber, and have a group meditation there, Thoth?"

"Yes, let's ascend to the Queen's Chamber, Master Yeshua," Thoth replied in a voice that spoke of his willingness to accommodate the Master's request. "I am the architect and Master builder of this pyramid and the two pyramids next to it. This pyramid was constructed with an accuracy level of being square within a couple inches on each side. Since the 51.52 pyramid angle resonates exactly with the human heart, we can consider it a love machine of sorts!"

"Also, you will not notice, but in the Kings Chamber we were in is directly in line with the apex of this pyramid, and that increases the energy of love you felt. The Queen's Chamber, however, is located some distance off the center of the apex, but it is closer thereto...making it immensely powerful as well!"

As we were entering the Queen's Chamber, Yeshua shared his perception of this chamber and noted, "I can feel there is a more feminine energy in this chamber—that of the Sophia Christ—the Sophia God!"

"Rabboni, I felt the same thing... I feel immersed in love," I exclaimed, "but I must ask, what is the Sophia Christ and the Sophia God?

"Sophia refers to the feminine and so Sophia Christ, is the feminine Christ, manifested in its God-realized nature. The Sophia God is the feminine aspects of God... directly related to LOVE and LIGHT," Yeshua explained in a clear and understandable manner. "Because of the inherent receptive nature of women, which comes from their feminine energy, they have the innate ability to Love!"

In the Shadow of a Master

Dr. Robert J. Newton

"Wow," I replied in an amazed and grateful tone, "I never considered any of that before now!"

All the while, Thoth just soaked in our comments and had a bemused smile upon his face. When there was a break in our conversation he noted, "Yeshua and James... you are the most perceptive of all the visitors I have accommodated in this pyramid—including my high priests. I am honored you have visited me...I am blessed by your presence! I know you will do great things in this world as way-showers...and I sense you will guide many people to connect with Osiris and Yahweh...God itself!"

Yeshua decided there was much benefit to meditate in the sarcophagus of the King's Chamber of the Great Pyramid, thus, we spent many weeks deepening our level and experiences therein. We both progressed in this skill, but as you might expect, Yeshua mastered being able to meditate at the level of delta brainwaves, which is equivalent to sleep, and yet, sleep Yeshua did not. He reached such a deep state on the Djed meditation of the Ida-Pingala, it took him to the most extreme level of kundalini...pure, raw, God energy! That is how Thoth described it.

Every once and while, Thoth would join us in deep meditation. He was in awe of what Yeshua was achieving inside the Great Pyramid, and he expressed such.

"Shalom, Thoth," Yeshua replied, "would you please take us to Thebes so we can experience the Temple of Man, of which I believe you were also the architect and Master builder thereof?"

"Yes, of course. I was hoping you would take some time to visit another of my Master pieces—built to glorify our God!" Thoth replied with a satisfied look on his face. We can sail down the Nile River to Thebes, in a felucca sailboat. I will have someone attend to your donkey; in the few days we are there. Let's proceed there, directly, alright?"

"We are blessed to have your guidance and accommodation, Master Thoth," Yeshua replied with a look of satisfaction on his face, again mirroring Thoth by nodding his head up and down.

During their sailing on the felucca, the sun on the water on the Nile made for a relaxed and special feeling, which enveloped us, along with our captain of our ship. Date Palms graced the shore of the Nile, and on either side, there were fields of vegetables, beans, grains, corn, and citrus. Since we left in the afternoon, nightfall was upon us within a few hours. All the while and into late in the evening, Thoth explained why he felt it was necessary to clarify the nuances of the Djed meditation Yeshua had completed in his time travel to the center of the Milky Way Galaxy, where he arrived at the land of Seth.

He also talked about the temple complex at Karnack in Thebes and shared how it was constructed as energy generators that expressed the energy of God. He further discussed how The Temple of Man was constructed as a complete representation of the human body, including the chakra energy centers that are part of a human form, which distribute God's life force energy, throughout the body.

Late into the night, I fell asleep on the felucca, while Thoth and Yeshua continued sharing deep spiritual insights with each other. I awoke in the morning, at first sun, and began my morning meditation, as did Yeshua and Thoth, as well. Their meditation lasted about an hour. I watched them slowly come out of the meditative state, and Thoth, as he gave me a handful of dates to eat for breakfast, casually queried, "James, were you able to assimilate the incredible meditations you had in the King's Chamber?"

In the Shadow of a Master

Dr. Robert J. Newton

Grateful for Master Thoth's concern for me, I replied, "Yes! I had some incredible flashbacks of my sojourn to a planet where I had incarnated many times before. You know, my breathing stopped during that meditation and excursion, and I had an intense energy of Love overtake my body. And my face...it felt as though it was on fire...consumed in flames, yet it was not.

With a touch of light laughter, Thoth responded, "Ah-ha! You experienced the extremely intense energy of the Djed, James. Scanning the wise mind of your Rabboni, Yeshua, I think you will experience something similar in Kriya Kundalini Yoga Pranayam, when you visit India. So much fun you will have there, as your thirst for learning and insight might never be quenched...a quality much to be sought and emulated!"

"I must say that am honored by the caring insights and knowledge you have shared with me, Master Thoth. I knew Rabboni Yeshua would expand my consciousness and open my heart on our expeditious journey, but I never thought we would meet someone as wise and experienced as you on our expedition. I am so honored to have your acquaintance and guidance!"

"I, too, feel blessed being in the presence of seekers of God, like you and Rabboni Yeshua, James. We are close to docking in Thebes so let me share some things with you and your Master Yeshua about the Temple of Man."

"If you enter this temple slowly, you are going to have your intuition opened widely, but if you progress post haste, you will most likely miss a lot of things that will enrich your consciousness and life, so please heed my words! Those who enter in haste, will never have the full taste or know the true import and impact of this temple!"

In the Shadow of a Master

Dr. Robert J. Newton

As we disembarked from the felucca and proceeded to the Temple of Man, Yeshua shared further guidance for me as he instructed, "I agree with everything Master Thoth has shared with us and I would add, when we get to the temple, there will be huge stone statues of Ramses and his wife, Nefertiti, who were enlightened leaders during their incarnation on Earth...please take the time to honor their presence, before you enter!"

As we arrived at the entrance to The Temple of Man, I was reviewing what Yeshua and Thoth had shared with me. As I acknowledged Ramses and Nefertiti, I slowly entered the temple, which no longer had its roof, and immediately started having visions of myself in a previous incarnation as a priest in the Temple of Man and seeing rooms which were no longer delineated inside the temple. I also started feeling the seven major energy centers in my body, known as Chakras, being infused with more energy, as well—in the crown of my head, in the brow/third eye/pineal gland, in my throat, in my heart, in my diaphragm, in my solar plexus and my root, at my tailbone.

Confused and unsure of what I was experiencing, I asked Yeshua, "Is it possible for me to see things that might have existed in the past or am I hallucinating about feeling my chakras activated, as I move through The Temple of Man?"

"That depends on how you define a hallucination," Yeshua replied, authoritatively. "By my understanding and knowledge, a hallucination is accessing something from a parallel or higher Dimension of consciousness, and it is also related to one's level of personal consciousness—where the mind is quieted and is able to access information beyond the daily affairs of life and experience the full bliss of being at one with God…and…well, James, there is just nothing more important than that!"

Hearing all of this, Thoth confirmed what Yeshua shared with me as he expounded, "What Master Yeshua shared with you James, I completely agree with and confirm. The Temple of Man was arranged by me with a layout called sacred geometry. This means everything is related together in a sacred layout, which allows people's minds to access psychic abilities that are from a higher consciousness. It allows people to see past and future events: it facilitates being able to know things about people through telepathy, which, you understand, is purely a mental communication with the ability to discern things about them without having to question them. Learn to trust and follow these things, James, because your life and base of spiritual knowledge will be greatly enhanced It is clear to see you have had a mind and consciousness expanding experience here, and it has made you much more alive and aware and empowered with God!"

Yeshua's experience in The Temple of Man, vastly exceeded mine, as he began levitating in the temple, enveloped in an intense orb of light, which completely surrounded his body and head. The priests that were in the temple, already knew Yeshua was extraordinary beyond all others, were as stunned to silence, and in awe of this, as was I.

Yeshua and I spent several months experiencing the magic in the Temple of Man and the temples in the Karnak complex in Thebes. The energy in the sandstone columns of the temples in Thebes was intense, especially when I just relaxed and let it flow through my body. The sandstone contained small quartz crystals that released this elevated field of energy. When Yeshua and I would extend our hands between these columns, with our hands ninety degrees to our arms, it would charge and enhance the energy fields in our bodies. This amazing phenomenon, which Thoth tipped us off about, became an addicting experience for us.

Thoth also suggested to Yeshua that we back track to The Temple of Abydos, sailing northward on the felucca. Yeshua sensed there might be value in this idea and agreed that we proceed to Abydos in the morning, for a day's journey, thereto.

As we subsequently bedded down in an inn well- known to Thoth, I slipped off to sleep, whilst Yeshua and Thoth, not needing sleep, had a deep discussion about the many special wonders in Egypt. They also discussed Thoth's *Book of the Dead*, and the mysteries of the myriad nuances of taking a body into a state of immortality, transiting through the underworld. Yeshua opened a discussion about Balaam, a Moabite, considered to be the one who teaches us Jews the way to reach eternity.

Then, Thoth shared the *Corpus Hermeticum*, which he authored, that discusses the divine right of humans to live in a state of immortality, without having to die first. I awoke as Thoth was dispensing this information and found myself intrigued by the possibility—and even our right—to transcend the state of death. This made me so elated I had assented to Yeshua' s invitation to journey on to other lands and learn from other traditions, beyond just the Torah and the Kabbalah. I could never have imagined anything like this would have been revealed to us on trek to other lands!

Since I was awake, Thoth and Yeshua decided they would get an early start on our journey back up the Nile River, to the Temple of Abydos. We ate some dried fish and dates...all under a sunrise filled with the red, orange, and yellow colors of daybreak—a sublime sight and an absolute delight to view. I stood there for a moment, struck by how amazing the works of The Lord were!

We were blessed with the best current of the Nile and favorable winds that filled the sails of the felucca and by late afternoon we arrived at a port, close to Abydos, where we rented donkeys for the ten-mile ride to the temple...staying the night in a small inn. I seemed to be developing a pattern, where I slept while Yeshua and Thoth discussed the *Corpus Hermeticum* and Thoth's *Samardine Tablet*, also known as the *Emerald Tablet*.

Yeshua was especially intrigued at how the *Samardine Tablet* discussed how all levels of creation were inextricably interrelated, as designed by the Creator, itself, which he already knew but got a different perspective. Even more impressive, was how Thoth deciphered the true nature of man in the *Corpus Hermeticum*, where he exhorted mankind to claim their right to be immortal and not subject to decay and the ravages of death, as we had been taught and believed were inevitable.

When the first light of morning appeared, we made a short trek to the temple and Thoth took us to an interior room in the Temple of Abydos that held intriguing carved-relief objects. Neither Yeshua nor I had seen anything like them, so Thoth explained what he was showing us. "There are two pictures of aircraft, that ply the skies and one picture of an underwater craft. Now, I know we do not see these craft in our lands, or so you would believe, yet people from the stars have been coming to earth since time immemorial, at least in the aircraft, and sometimes time portals, like a wheel within a wheel, described in Ezekiel 1:4-16, which creates a time warp...a transit portal in which to visit other lands and Dimensions. They brought this knowledge here. I am one of those star people...as is Yeshua...as are you, James!"

"Great wisdom and spiritual practices technology were brought from these stars, including Sirius "A", Sirius "B", Orion, Pleiades, Andromeda, and Nibiru, the last of which is in our solar system. We also need to remember that the people of Seth have visited Earth for billions of years!"

I'm quite sure both Thoth and Yeshua noticed my eyes grow large...and watched deep furrows burrow in my forehead, as I pondered things of which I had no previous knowledge. I finally checked my emotions and asked Yeshua, "Master, is this all true?"

"Yes, James, all this is true and so much more," Yeshua replied in an assuring tone, accompanied by the now characteristic moving his head up and down. "Thoth has revealed to me Nibiru is in our solar system, on an elliptical orbit and hence, it spends very little time proximate to the rest of the planets in our solar system, but exists, nonetheless."

This was so much for me to process that I became silent, in an attempt to make sense of what I was being exposed to. No one in Judea or any other part of Israel or Palestine, had ever mentioned anything like this, nor had I seen anything like it in the books or pictures found in the synagogues.

Yeshua then broke through my silence to confirm what Thoth had shared and addressed me, saying "This is the quandary in which mankind has been placed. The obsession of man being a sinner and cursed from time immemorial—into antiquity—by the acts of Adam and Eve and also Adam and Lilith, have obscured the great divinity in which we have been created, revealed in the first two chapter of Genesis, irrespective of whatever acts were committed by our ancestors."

"Do you really believe that God is so pernicious as to punish and curse us for the acts of someone else, like Adam and Eve...for acts that we did not commit ourselves? Would you do the same with your children? Would any parent do this—punish their children for acts committed by others? Fundamentally, we are all God's beloved children, divinely created as in the 7th Names of God from the "72 Names of God, *Aleph Kaf Aleph...* restoring perfection to Earth! Eventually, we will be preaching to the masses of Israel, James, and I will be sharing with them that which I have shared with you in our private audience. Now it is time for us to move onward and upward to Greece, James!"

CHAPTER 5

TRAVELING TO GREECE AND LEARNING THERE WAS NOT A
LOT OF GREASE THERE...BUT OLIVES APLENTY, AND GOAT
MILK AND HONEY.

TIME PASSED QUICKLY AS we engaged in consciousness expanding
experiences and encounters with God in Egypt, and our travel to
Greece, which Thoth had agreed was a good choice, because he had
personally been there many times. Thoth suggested it would greatly
benefit us if we were to contact Apollo in Greece, near Athens. He
even hinted Apollo might get us an audience with the Oracle of
Delphi, which was a revered source of spiritual information and
insights. Then Thoth decided it would be fun to travel with us to
Greece.

I saw Yeshua's eyes shine and twinkle when Thoth mentioned
the Oracle and that he would accompany us, although as the novice
in this journey, I had no idea what either of them were discussing in
reference to the Oracle of Delphi or why it was important. I felt

fortunate to have quickly learned to trust Yeshua, implicitly, because he was always true to his word, unlike any one I had known before. He always exuded confidence and that is because he always did what he claimed he would and even much more, beyond that!

Thoth shared with us his vast knowledge of the great philosophers of Greece, the most venerated being—Plato, who also tutored the well-known Aristotle. Speaking of Plato, Thoth explained, "Plato was respected widely for his knowledge of ethics, cosmology, and metaphysics. His journey into metaphysics was in fact one of his great contributions to Greece and the World. Plato maintained, as do I, that that which appears to be physical...dense matter, has as its essence a form...an energy... an ether, which comprises its real nature."

"That is quite germane to us because meta means 'beyond' and physics means 'physical', so it means beyond the physical, to the realm of energy or ethers. Plato lived in Athens, Greece, yet the average citizens had little knowledge of his great knowledge and insights. They were more familiar with his work, *The Republic*, which discussed government and how the citizens of that government should act to ensure all actions are more just and fair to its citizens."

Thoth alerted Yeshua to the possibility of meeting with Apollo and the Oracle of Delphi, which was deemed not as one person or soul, but rather a group of them. Thoth invoked the presence of Apollo, who was venerated as he who was associated with the sun, light, and knowledge. Yeshua spent some time discussing metaphysics with Apollo, which seemed to expand the understanding of both men. Apollo agreed to introduce Yeshua and Thoth to the Oracle of Delphi, an honor reserved for the most knowledgeable and wise beings on Earth. Yeshua humbly thanked Thoth for his initial intervention on his behalf, which set all that followed into action.

The Oracle of Delphi was an aggregation of the best philosophers and mathematicians in Greece, from the past and present. This included deceased philosophers like Plato and Socrates, who were held in the highest esteem for their vast knowledge and wisdom. Also included in the Oracle was Pythagoras, who was known for his advanced understanding of mathematics and geometry, which he had learned from the ancient Egyptians. Asclepius, the Greek God of medicine and doctors, was also part of the Oracle, and was known for his vast knowledge of herbal remedies and lucid daydream healing, and he was believed to be the son of Apollo, an extraterrestrial, who mated with an Earth woman. Asclepius' student and follower, Apollonius of Tyana, likewise carried on the healing knowledge of Asclepius. Hippocrates was also revered as a healer in Greece, as well, but according to Apollo, not in the league of Asclepius.

Philosopher's Herodotus, Pericles, and Plato had a wealth of knowledge about the large sunken continent, Atlantis, much of it handed down to them through an oral tradition. They knew Atlantis was a very high-tech society, although it seems lost in the mists of time, relegated by most citizens of Greece as wild speculation. Socrates, the teacher of Plato—and Plato himself, as well as Euclid of Megara, and Herodotus had knowledge of the Phoenix, a fiery bird like an Eagle, which regenerated itself every five hundred years. Herodotus said he had never seen the death or rebirth of the Phoenix, but it was well known and accepted on the Island of Phoenicia. The long-told and fascinating stories of the Phoenix were especially compelling to Yeshua, because he had already learned from the Essenes about the immortality of humans, and considered this as the normal state of man, instead of deterioration and death, which was in vogue all over the Earth.

Thoth then offered a vast collective of information about the Phoenix. As he shared with Yeshua and James, he explained, "There is something in the Greek astrology that gives us insight into the Phoenix, which just happens to be part of the three stages or aspects of the astrology of Scorpio. Persons born under the sign of Scorpio, begin their life as seekers of high knowledge and understanding, yet can be deadly if they are crossed, since the Scorpio (scorpion) does not hesitate to inflict its venom upon any unevolved soul, which may inflict themselves upon him with false knowledge and debased standards.

As the Scorpio grows in understanding, it ascends its second stage of the Eagle. The Eagle is known to be a lonely soul like the scorpion; however, it learns to soar above many of the travails on Earth, only becoming Earth bound on the occasions when it swoops down to take prey for sustenance."

"After forty years of living, the Eagle must either contemplate death, because its feathers are too matted, and its beak and talons become so curved as to be useless in the catching and killing of prey, so as to have food to survive."

Thoth enjoyed the rapt attention he saw on the faces of Yeshua and James as he continued his narrative. "Yet, if the Eagle plucks out its feathers, and then grinds down its beak and talons, it will regenerate new feathers and talons and a beak. As you might have contemplated, this is like a dress rehearsal of sorts for the third stage of Scorpio, where the Phoenix ultimately is consumed in its own flames and regenerated therefrom from its ashes. In the Vedic Indian lore, ashes are considered a holy and regenerative substance. There is also something else similar in India called Kayakalpa, which uses Kriya Kundalini Pranayam(a) and rare and powerful herbs, as well as holy ash, to regenerate a declining human body."

"It is of utmost importance to understand that at least a number of of these philosophers, healers, and mathematicians were of human, extraterrestrial hybrid births, including as I mentioned, Asclepius, Pythagoras, and Plato and a few others, like Hercules and Mercury." Thoth suddenly became very animated as he attempted to give more power to his story, saying, "It might have been the higher origins of their births, which accounted for their great healing insights and powers and philosophical and mathematical genius."

Without advance notice to Yeshua or James, the next morning Thoth came to Yeshua and declared, "The Oracle of Delphi is ready to have an audience with you, Master, and is most insistent you attend! We need to sail to the Gulf of Corinth, and then ascend to Mt. Parnassus, the location of Apollo's Temple of the Oracle."

A great light of joy covered the face of Yeshua, as he responded, "Thank you, Thoth. And James, we need to be on our way to meet the Oracle of Delphi. Let's find a ship so we can sail there with Thoth, from Athens! Hopefully, our donkey will have its sea legs!"

In affirmation, I subconsciously nodded as Yeshua so frequently did…gently, slowly, up and down with my head…and we proceeded the Temple of Delphi. The trip was sunny, and we had tranquil seas, as are so often experienced in the Mediterranean Sea. As we proceeded thereto, we ascended a cliff, and as we entered, therein, we could see a fiery flame at one end of the Parthenon.

In the Shadow of a Master

Dr. Robert J. Newton

When we finally arrived at our destination, with Thoth in tow, Yeshua bowed his head in reverence. I was not sure what he was doing, but watching him, I figured it was an honorable acknowledgement to the Oracle of Delphi, Pythia... the high priestess. It seemed to my intuition that Yeshua was establishing a link with the Oracle. There were no audible words spoken by the Oracle or Yeshua, but I sensed a telepathy of sorts...an exchange from mind to mind, with questions and comments. There was a sanguine look on Yeshua' s face, which was noticed by Thoth, as well. After about an hour of this meeting, Yeshua bowed to Pythia, and then turned away and began to leave the Temple of Delphi.

As Yeshua took this all in, his eyes and face began to glow and with Thoth and me listening, he declared, "I received some very revealing information and insights, Thoth and James, and there is a greater depth to this civilization in Greece than I ever imagined! This is just more evidence our Creator/God, made us perfect and immortal, as per Aleph Kaf Aleph and the perfection bestowed upon us from this name—and Hey Resh Chet, which is the light of God that is infused indelibly into our bodies, and through which we are inexorably connected."

"You would have been fascinated, James! Pythia, the Oracle, was accessing information from many sources, and quickly and easily collating the information into something coherent and intelligible. I am sure Plato was at my audience with the Pythia, as was Asclepius and Pythagoras. They seemed to weave science, healing, and philosophy into a far bigger picture than either of these separate disciplines, alone!"

I was all ears as Yeshua continued, deep in sharing his thoughts. "I was immensely curious and asked the Pythia about the most advanced Greek healer. She graciously noted she would circle back to Asclepius, and stated he was the most gifted of all the healers of the Middle East, Europe, India, and China. She also revealed he was a Master herbalist and known to attain healings for patients for all manner of sickness and disease. The history she shared made note that Asclepius had an epiphany and realized he could heal patients better and faster by putting them in a lucid daydream state. His success with this process of putting the patients into a higher state of consciousness, in a state of atonement (at one ment) with their Father-Mother God—and allowed the patients to heal themselves. Pythia mentioned how her belief that the phrase, *Physician, heal thyself,* was wrongly attributed to Hippocrates, but was really from Asclepius.

Amazed at the depth of the knowledge Yeshua had culled from Pythia, Thoth observed, with great respect and awe, "I know you are already a great healer, Rabboni, but what you have learned today will be eventually unleased on humanity, and there is going to be a lot of healing occurring...wherever you go. I am in fervent anticipation of what you will learn in Tibet and India, Yeshua!"

"Thank you so much for being the go between for Pythia and me, Thoth," Yeshua was literally bubbling over with his gratitude as he extended an invitation to Thoth. "If you would like to accompany us to Tibet and India, please know your presence and guidance would be most appreciated!"

"Let make it happen, Yeshua! I would be honored to continue with you and James on your journey," Thoth responded in a most appreciate manner. "Are you going by ship or are you planning to take advantage of light travel, via a Merkabah?"

In the Shadow of a Master

Dr. Robert J. Newton

"I believe we should light travel, Thoth, and we will bring our donkey in tow," Yeshua replied with a smug look on his face, raising his eyebrows, and offering me a wry smile.

"That is great with me, Yeshua. I was mentally communicating with your donkey and found out he had only three legs when you acquired him, and you put the energy together to manifest a fourth leg, for which he is most appreciative," Yeshua and I both glanced at Thoth and saw there a look on his face confirming that he had let the Abyssinian cat out of the bag. "Let's bed down in the Inn, tonight, and then contemplate our next journey, in the morning."

CHAPTER 6

OFF TO THE ENCHANTED AND FAR AWAY LANDS OF TIBET AND NEPAL.

WE SET OUR SIGHTS on the Yarlung Valley, on the Tibetan Plateau, at a Buddhist temple where the Buddhists had established a beachhead 500 years before.

In the morning, after a quick breakfast of dates, the three of us and our donkey were connected, hand to hand and hand to hoof. I watched as Yeshua and Thoth began accumulating the God force energy, which was necessary for a group Merkabah to move at the speed of light from one place to another. The process took a second or two to light travel, and I had grown comfortable knowing there would always be a state of disorientation, moving at such a mega speed.

Yeshua then turned his attention to me to offer a word of caution. "These Buddhists are of a different religion than we, James, but the only relevant thing here is whether they are devoted to the Lord God. Their leader Buddha Gautama was and currently is the obsession of the Buddhist monks who spend hours in meditation... picturing him as a means to the ultimate goal to honor and learn more about God. Is there really anything else, as important, even though we approach this differently, without idols?"

Thoth then interjected with a few salient comments, as he shared, "The Buddhist monks will focus on one thing during their meditation, often Gautama Buddha. They get their focus to where they can meditate for hours at a time, as what Yeshua just shared. It going to be cold tonight, so the monks are going to don wet sheets at dark, let those sheets freeze, and then use their prana...their chi...the life force of God, to melt those frozen sheets and return themselves to an amazing state of warmth and deep meditative concentration. We have been invited to participate in this ceremony, Yeshua and James so..."

Evening came and I found myself experiencing a lot of trepidation about whether I could melt a frozen sheet with only the life force of God, but I declared, "This seems vastly beyond my abilities, but I will give it a go, Yeshua!"

"Just concentrate on the Djed meditation we practiced in Egypt, James, and things will go right for you James." His voice was confident and assuring tone of voice and he continued to reassure me, saying. "I am very much looking forward to this, James...it will be loads of fun! We will use the force and omnipresent energy of God and infuse that into our bodies to melt the ice. Practically, this has many applications in the rest of our life! It is an exercise in concentrating your mind and focus so as to accumulate a lot of

Chi/God energy! It gives us a measure of how tight we are with God!"

The ceremony reflected an interesting contrast of Yeshua, Thoth, and James who had long hair and varying degrees of beards and mustaches, whereas the Buddhist monks' heads were shaved and without facial hair. Thoth felt compelled to explain this dichotomy, noting, "The Buddhist monks have no hair or facial hair as they feel this humbles them and makes them more supplicant to God, whereas as we know that long hair and facial hair is like a cosmic antenna, which allows us to attract and amplify the power of our Lord God. We can use this to our advantage, to magnify the force of God in our bodies, James!"

The Buddhist monks and Yeshua and Thoth were quick to build the God force energy in their bodies to melt the ice on the sheets, in a fifteen-degree Fahrenheit temperature. Alas! I was the last of the group to melt his sheets, but melt them I did, much to my satisfaction. I boldly declared, "That is a real confidence booster for me! Thanks to you Rabboni and Thoth, for giving me the support and confidence to pull this off."

The two Masters smiled at my remarks, and approvingly acknowledged my achievement. By now, Thoth was also into the nodding of heads up and down; each wore a smile on his glowing face and was immersed in an intense field of light.

I noticed the twinkle flashing in Thoth's eyes as he announced, "Tomorrow we are going to watch a group of monks levitate a multi-ton stone up the side of a cliff. We are going to be the first foreigners to witness this feat. It is important to observe this with an understanding it is not done for ego or to impress anybody, rather, it is an exercise in the monks working together to do something, seemingly impossible and probably not even logistically possible with pulleys and levers. Tonight, we will bed in the Yarlung Monastery, close to Mt. Kailash."

My reaction was quick! I didn't stop to think before the words tumbled from me. "This will be an incredible event to witness...if the Buddhist monks can pull this off!"

The next day, after a lot of mediation in the Yarlung Buddhist Tempe, Yeshua, Thoth, a large group of monks, and I walked to a vertical chasm and cliff. The monks seated themselves at the edge of the chasm and cliff and began their mantra...a specific repetitive prayer...in a split tone bass voice, starting each mantra with Aum.

While engaging in the mantra, the monks focused their attention on a multi-ton boulder and as the energy behind their mantra began to build, the huge boulder began to levitate upward. This process continued until the monks rested the boulder on a ledge on the vertical cliff.

My eyes were bulging out of my head, as I strained to process what I had just witnessed. I moved my attention toward Yeshua, and asked, "What just happened here, Master? It did not take the monks that long to levitate the stone...or did my eyes betray me?

Your eyes are fine, James, and what you just witnessed was millions of microscopic energy particles, which are the fundamental essence of God and all people and things on Earth, including the huge boulder, were stimulated by the mantra, and this energy made these particles move faster, and became more energy than matter. That is how the boulder levitated up the side of the cliff," Yeshua responded, sure of his answer.

In the Shadow of a Master

Dr. Robert J. Newton

Then Thoth, verifying what Yeshua had just explained to me, provided additional information, saying, "That is exactly how we moved the multi-ton blocks of stone up the pyramids, in the process of their construction. This is exactly how we built the Great Pyramid you were inside, James. We repeated an Egyptian mantra, *A Ka Dua*, over and over until the blocks of stone levitated upward!"

"Thanks, Thoth. I was going to ask you about the task of moving those multi-ton blocks of stone upward and into place. There was a theory about this going round Israel...that there were tens of thousands of Jewish slaves who pulled those stones up ramps to get them placed!"

"Yes, we know all about that fairy tale, James. You would be interested to know we tried that but the higher the course of stones, the steeper the ramp—and it would not have been feasible even with 100,000 laborers to attempt it, because there would not be space enough for all those laborers."

In honor of their visit, the Buddhist monks arrayed many prayer flags in honor of Yeshua, Thoth, and me. I am sure we all three felt honored by the flags, which were flying as we departed to Nepal. They also created some elaborate colored sand mandalas, in honor of us. We decided to walk with our donkey in tow, so we could spend some time in Nepal, and visit with more Buddhist monks, at Bouddanath Monastery, east of Katmandu, which, of course, Thoth highly recommended.

The valleys between the huge Himalaya mountains were passable because it was springtime, but we faced the extreme of temperatures which were below freezing at night, and the patches of snow strewn about.

45

In the Shadow of a Master

Dr. Robert J. Newton

So, with nothing more than sandals and heavy robes, we moved along at a brisk pace, using what we learned from the Buddhist monks, in melting the ice off a sheet, to keep ourselves warm. After two days of travel, we arrived at the Maya Devi Temple in Lumbini, Nepal, where Buddha is known to have found enlightenment. Because of this, all Buddhists revered this particular temple. We introduced themselves to the head monk and could feel the intense energy of love that Buddha had previously imprinted into this temple...five hundred years earlier.

Yeshua, immersing himself in Buddha's love, was moved to remark, "A lot of people are overly obsessed with their religion and that religion being the only true and correct one. But verily, I say unto you, God is no respecter of religions, and cares only about the love his subjects express to their fellow men. That is the true measure of a man or woman...how much of the Father's love they share and dispense!"

"This is more easily facilitated if we attract and become God's light. We really cannot have one without the other! Unfortunately, governments seem to want to obscure this reality...to muddle things because they have a compulsive need to control their subjects and try to make themselves a deity—yet they are not divinely suited or qualified to be such! I think right now, what we need is a deep, extended session of meditation, in the manner of the Djed meditation!"

In the midst of Buddhist monks inside the Maya Devi Temple, we formed a small circle and began an extended breathing meditation, which infused our bodies with more of the light of God. After about an hour, I ended my meditation and noticed Yeshua and Thoth were so infused with the light of God they were glowing. The glow did not surprise me, but I think seeing them levitating a foot off the ground did! There they sat suspended midair, in the Lotus meditation position, with their index finger, middle finger, and ring finger conjoined with their thumbs in each hand, much like the Buddhist monks were doing, as well. This position of the fingers, which was an advanced mudra, created an energy circuit connecting their crowns, pineal gland/third eye, and root chakra in the tail bone, via their spinal columns and the cerebrospinal fluid that connected them contiguously.

Thoth knew cerebrospinal fluid increased in a body, during deep meditation, and this allowed someone meditating to access the highest levels of God, because it had an extra infusion of God energy or prana, connecting the brain/mind to the spinal column to the root/tailbone, via the cerebra spinal fluid. I watched as Yeshua and Thoth intensified their meditation by repeating Om/Aum, sub-vocally, which unleashed even more light and energy inside their bodies. Yeshua had an expression of sheer bliss on his face, with a subtle smile dominating it. Right before my very eyes he became a most intense bright light, indeed!

After two hours, Yeshua and Thoth ended their meditations closely at the same time. Amazed at what he had just witnessed, my curiosity got the best of me. I just had to ask, "What did you feel during your meditation, Yeshua? You were not only levitating but had a look of bliss on your face!"

"I was lost in the light and love of our God," Yeshua proclaimed with an assured confidence. "I felt an at-one-ment...a melding with God. I came to a deep and abiding knowing...that I could do and accomplish anything in that state! I am even more certain now; this is the secret to happiness and success...our connection to the light and love of God."

Thoth then shared the insights of his meditation. "I agree with Yeshua...we were in a deeply connected state with God. Being in this temple, with the monks, who have dedicated their lives in service to Buddha and God, definitely enriched our meditation greatly, James! The imprints of their previous meditations created a discernable field of energy that pervades this temple!"

It was close to dinner time for the monks, and they invited us to join them in their meal, which was rice, beans, and vegetables. There was an intuitive sharing of mutual admiration that occurred telepathically, between the Buddhist monks, Yeshua, Thoth, and me.

Since they lived a cloistered life, with little contact with the outside world, the leader of the monks, Chodron, which means the light of Dharma, was telepathically asking questions about the whereabouts of his three visitors. Master Chodron then telepathically directed his thoughts to us, In Buddhism, dharma is the nature of reality and universal truth; he knew we do not just circumscribe this with Buddhism alone, because we have trained our minds to seek truth from any and all sources!

Yeshua then exclaimed, "I, for one, am most grateful to have been blessed to be in your presence, Chodron. I have never seen such a deep, disciplined search for God, displayed by any humans, even in my own land of Israel and the teaching of the Essenes!"

Thoth was also compelled to share his feelings and noted, "I must agree with Master Yeshua. I am very humbled to be in your presence, Chodron, and that of your monks. Their pervasive energy uplifts this temple with a definite connection to our creator God"

In the Shadow of a Master

Dr. Robert J. Newton

The response was warming to my ears—and heart— as, with a deep reverence Chodron sub-vocally asserted, *feel free to sleep in our temple tonight and as long as you desire. We are honored to be in the presence of three men of God!*

Yeshua, Thoth, and I each honorably bowed our heads in acknowledgement of the invitation from Chodron, each grateful for the offer.

"Let's sleep on this and then make some plans in the morning," Yeshua declared.

Thoth and I acknowledged this with a nod of our heads, and we were off to sleep on our lamb's wools bed rolls. As usual, however, Yeshua and Thoth spent most of the night in deep meditation and contemplation, whereas I spent most of the night in lucid daydreams, sleep, and dreams.

The morning came with little warning, other than a brilliantly colored sunrise breaking across the horizon, which awakened James and broke night long meditations of Yeshua and Thoth, who were both of the opinion it could do them nothing but good to soak in the love and enlightenment of the Buddha. Hence, we unexpectedly decided there was merit in associating and meditating with the Buddhist monks at the Bouddanath Temple in Katmandu, Nepal. So, we spent another two weeks there, most of the time in deep meditation. I did a lot of observing and noticed as each day passed how the aura of light surrounding Yeshua became brighter and more intense.

Yeshua had a dream…a lucid daydream in which he had a type of meditation, similar to the Djed, which was taught to him and me, by Thoth. He was certain we needed to depart to Northern India, in

In the Shadow of a Master

Dr. Robert J. Newton

Punjab Province. When Yeshua telepathed his intent to go to India to Thoth, and Thoth acknowledged such with a nod of his head, I knew something was up. My intuition was spot on and I was not at all surprised to learn we likely would be departing for India, after breakfast.

Yeshua, Thoth, and I found audience with Chodrin, and with our eyes and telepathic intent, thanked him profusely for providing a safe haven for us in Nepal. It was evident Chodrin had grown close to Yeshua and Thoth, yet with no indication of sorrow, intuitively shared his thoughts with us, graciously thanked us for our association, and wished us a safe voyage. All the people around, including Chodron's monks, put their hands together over their hearts and bowed their heads to us and to each other.

Yeshua, knowing one of the Tibetan monks had been ill and in severely declining health, walked over to the monk, who was meditating, put his hands above his head, wherefrom came streams of intense light, and in Hebrew, declared, "Beloved monk…go and sin no more. Your worth to God is considerable." Little surprise that almost immediately, a surge of energy entered the monk's body and he returned to a state of radiant health. With tears of joy streaming down his face, the monk kissed Yeshua' s feet. Yeshua humbly bowed to him and began to depart the temple.

And with that, Yeshua was joined by Thoth, and me, and we started on our journey to India. As we were departing, we glanced around to see Chodron quickly following Yeshua. As he made his way to the master's side, Chodron hugged Yeshua and bowed his head to him, showing the greatest respect and reverence. After a moment of quiet acceptance for the gesture, in deference, Yeshua exclaimed, "Shalom…blessings to you all!"

CHAPTER 7

OFF TO INDIA...THE LAND DIVINE.

FROM KATMANDU, NEPAL, THE pilgrims made their way through sharp mountain passes through the Himalayas to Varanasi and ancient temples devoted to Lord Shiva and Lord Vishnu. The journey took several days through a cold, snow filled landscape, between 9000-12000 feet.

Along the way, they encountered a man of great power and wisdom, Boganathar. Although unbeknownst to us at first, Boganathar was a Kriya Kundalini Yoga Avatar—a Satguru, if you will—and held in the highest esteem throughout India among the Holy Men, Hindu priests and in the order of Kriya Kundalini Yogis. This chance meeting would become a seminal event in the life of Jesus (Yeshua), as it would expose him to the guarded spiritual knowledge of Kriya Kundalini Yoga and Boganathur's teacher, Satguru Agastyar, who was likewise venerated among the spiritual elite in India.

In the Shadow of a Master

Dr. Robert J. Newton

Boganathar had immortalized his human body, through attaining the state of Soruba Samadhi, which meant he had transcended the ravages of death on Earth, needing neither breathing or food to sustain himself. His psychic abilities were highly-honed and fully developed, and while he could see a deep spiritual intent in the older Thoth, he was transfixed by the tremendous light—in a rainbow of colors—that visibly surrounded Yeshua's body, vastly beyond the distance of two feet. While on the trail to Varanasi, Boganathar and Yeshua began an intense melding of their minds through an intense telepathy. Boganathar knew where Yeshua was from and what he had learned to the point in time of their meeting. He intuited Yeshua had regenerated the leg on their donkey companion and healed an extremely sick Buddhist monk n Katmandu. He mentioned to the pilgrims, "I would like to take you to a Lord Shiva temple and a Lord Vishnu temple in Varanasi, as I know you will learn and experience a great benefit from being there!"

Yeshua, Thoth and I smiled and began—in unison—the now familiar slow nodding of heads, as affirmation to what Boganathar proposed. When the pilgrims would sleep just off the trail at night, Boganathar created an intense field of energy, he referred to as prana, that kept us warm and comfortable, throughout our meditation and nightly rest. He also manifested out of the ethers all the food we needed. This was done through an extended breathing meditation of Kriya Kundalini Pranayam(a).

Boganathar caught the attention and admiration of Thoth and Yeshua. Yeshua questioned him about this process of manifestation as he inquired, "Boganathar, I do believe this manifesting thing from the ethers is a twist on the healing process of body regeneration; am I right?"

"Yes, indeed, it is very much related to the process of healing and body regeneration, Yeshua," Boganathar replied in an authoritative voice, which I felt was the direct result of great experience and wisdom. "As I know you know, being a healer, Yeshua, you must first visualize what you want or need, and then put a lot of energy… Prana…the Spirit of the Lord, behind it, and it will be manifested into existence, as something tangible! If you would like, I believe we have time to teach all of you the Pranayam(a) meditation."

I was impressed by what Boganathar had done and then shared with us. Always the inquisitive one, I couldn't contain my next question: "Do you think I can learn to do that? I already know Yeshua can!"

"Yes, I believe my teacher, Agastyar, can give you some instruction in that just as he did for me. You will find him later in your journey through India, at the headwaters of the Ganges River, just below the Gangotri Glacier! In the meantime, I will teach you Pranayam(a) now."

"First, you must breathe as much as you can into your diaphragm, with your mouth closed, and then pull this breath up into your lungs. When you exhale, it must be twice as long as your inhaled breath, again, with your mouth closed. To exhale in this manner, you must put the tip of your tongue into your soft palate. You also need to turn your eyes upward without lifting your head upward. Do all these things and your lives will be changed much for the better and miracles will be available for you…at your fingertips…at any and all times!"

Yeshua and Thoth spent the night on the trail, engaging in Pranayam(a) along with Boganathar, while I, who was tired, slept soundly. In the morning, I began the Pranayam(a) breath protocols and started to notice the energy in my body increased and circulated with more intensity. I was particularly most grateful for increased energy; I even considered it my own personal miracle. After eating the traditional repast of dates, which were being carried by our donkey, we resumed our trek.

As we approached Varanasi, Boganathar instructed the group, saying, "Let me direct you to the Shiva Temple, as Lord Shiva is part of the trinity of God, as well as Lord Vishnu and Lord Brahma. These are three well-received aspects of God, but as Satguru Thirumoolar says in his book, *Thirumandiram*, 'There is but one God and Nandi is his name.' So, we must embrace that Nandi is associated with Lord Shiva and then encompasses the other two aspects of God, which are folded together! This then, Yeshua and James, you will find is similar to Yahweh, Elohim, and Jehovah, in your Hebrew tradition."

"I will leave your presence, for now, my friends," Boganathar proclaimed with respect, "but I just might join you later in your journey. Namaste and Namaska... be blessed in and by the presence of God!"

At the steps the Shiva Temple, the pilgrims entered thereto, and due to intense and dedicated connection to God, intense beams of white light shown through the bodies of Yeshua and Thoth. Yeshua's remark was purposeful as he stated, "This is evidence of our true connection to God as per the 59th Name of God from Exodus of the Torah, Hey Resh Chet...us being connected to the light. This source of light emanates from small electrical charges that comprise all creation—in innumerable amounts—created by our Creator-God, which permeate anything and everything!"

In the Shadow of a Master

byline
Dr. Robert J. Newton

The energy of the Shiva Temple was enabled and amplified by the gold leaf spires on the temple. The spires attracted the energy of God, which the Hindu's and Yogis called prana, to be magnified in the temple. The highly atom infused element, gold, added to this energy as well. As Yeshua became infused with this energy, a spectacle… a magical scene…began to occur.

The chief Hindu priest of the Shiva Temple, a Brahmin named Arjun, noticing the intense light phenomena surrounding Yeshua, walked toward us and clasped his hand over his heart and bowed to us. Thoth and I emulated Yeshua's reciprocal bow to our host. Arjun motioned for us to sit on some pillows as he began to sit, and soon we were all were seated in front of a statue of Lord Shiva. The energy the group created seemed to raise the roof of the temple, and everyone inside, therein, including the Hindu monks and temple visitors knew something special was occurring. After an extended, two-hour meditation, Arjun then motioned for us pilgrims to share dinner with him. As the temple cook summoned everyone in the temple to join in the evening feast, Yeshua began to telepath his thoughts to Brahmin Arjun, and share the journey we had undertaken and what we had experienced. How Arjun fascinated me as he intently took in what Yeshua shared with him, and expressed his gratitude for the insights Yeshua revealed, including the recent visitation with Buddhist priests, the melting of sheets, and the levitation of huge stones. He also invited us to stay at the temple as long as we desired.

Yeshua and Thoth agreed to this; however, Thoth suggested that we visit the Vishnu Temple in Varanasi, the next day, after their morning meditation session. Brahmin Arjun volunteered to lead us to the temple the next day and offered to introduce us to the head priest... the Brahmin of the Vishnu Temple, to which we assented and thanked him for his intervention.

Once again, Yeshua and Thoth spent the night in meditation and lucid dreaming, taking themselves into the higher Dimensions and Heavens beyond Earth. Their dedication made me feel ashamed for sleeping through the night and although I did sleep some, I started devoting more of the night to meditation, as did Yeshua and Thoth. In a strikingly short time, I noticed enhanced abilities to commune with God and the angels—giving me no shortage of delight!

When the first rays of light from the breaking morning Sun arrived, we all entered a deep state of meditation for two hours, although I could only muster about an hour of meditation. I still felt blessed and connected with the source of divinity that Yeshua and Thoth routinely experienced. On a whim—actually an intuitional hunch—Yeshua shared with Arjun that he would heal any priest or temple worshippers, if they would like to have a healing session for anyone who needed such. There was a priest with a severe intestinal disorder, who came forward for a healing encounter with Yeshua. Yeshua slowly turned his eyes upward and, with his head still level, a huge ball of light entered his body. Yeshua gently touched the priest, transferring the light he had invoked. After several minutes, a huge smile came across the priest's face, as the pain and suffering left his body immediately.

Next, a mother who had a small boy just a few years old, who had a deformed mouth asked Yeshua to make her son whole. Yeshua nodded with a sanguine smile on his face, and uttered, "Aleph Kaf Aleph...Lord God, please return your young creation here, back to the perfect state in which you created him!"

In the Shadow of a Master

Dr. Robert J. Newton

After a matter of mere seconds, the deformation of the boy's face disappeared, and he resumed his true form of a handsome young boy. With no other people in need of a healing, Yeshua and the rest of the group turned their attention to breakfast. After a breakfast of Naan bread, lentils, and basmati rice, eaten with Arjun and his priests, Yeshua, Thoth and I left the temple with Arjun leading the way to the Vishnu Temple in Varanasi.

The priest of this temple, Brahmin Hanaman, was both curious and honored to have Yeshua and Thoth visit his temple, since the entire town of Varanasi was abuzz with stories about the glowing presence of Yeshua and the stories of his amazing healing works in Tibet and Nepal and at the Temple of Shiva. By this time, Yeshua's healing works were known by everyone in Varanasi and there was a multitude of people and children seeking to be healed by him.

It was at this time the Indian people started calling Yeshua, St. Issa and Isha Masiha (Messiah/Prophet), Isha Putra (Son of God), as word of his healing works and the intense light around his body gained him notoriety and adulation.

Yeshua was concerned he might disrupt the Vishnu Temple, but his fear was assuaged by Brahmin Hanaman, who motioned to Yeshua to move to a line of people who were asking to be healed. Yeshua was not overwhelmed by the task before him; he was rather, more curious about all the ruckus he had stirred up. While he was more knowledgeable and competent in what he did than anyone else, Yeshua was always low key, and never sought attention to himself or his works. Nevertheless, he turned his eyes in an upward direction, as James had so often seen. James had come to learn the "Heavenly search" was to establish a direct connection with God, whom James also knew Yeshua acknowledged as his source and inspiration and the source power and cause of all healing. With all the people seeking his help, Yeshua decided to heal them all at once, regardless of their maladies. His upward turned eyes, while still looking ahead, brought an intense light into his body and into the entire temple. Shortly after, all the people were healed at once; many sobbed in joy to what happened to them as the long-experienced maladies fled their bodies. An equal number were seen profusely thanking Yeshua as they lavished praise upon him.

Yeshua, knowing he was only a channel of the energy of God and had no power or worth other than what he derived from God, told the multitude of people whom he had healed, "Please realize, I and my Father, God, are one and you are of the same lineage. This means, you are blessed far beyond anything you can comprehend with an unalterable connection to God...nothing can alter your godly origins"

After interacting with the throng of people, Yeshua went outside the temple, so as not to be noticed...where he then lavished his attention and praise upon the Lord God. He also gave thanks to Lord Shiva God, as well, realizing they were one and the same thing, as Jehovah. Yeshua would always say how differently things fit together and validated each other, in a state of non-duality of connectedness, where others concentrated on the differences between religions and philosophies. Likewise, Master Thoth had the same perspective and codified such in the *Smaragdine Tablet* also known as the *Emerald Tablet.*

Thoth went outside the Vishnu Temple, looking for Yeshua, and when he found him, he exclaimed, "That was a healing demonstration unlike any other I have ever witnessed before, Yeshua. The light of the Lord, streaming into your body was surely a sight to behold...I never thought it to be so intense and bright! In the Order of Kriya Kundalini Yoga, they would say you are infused with prana...Yagna or fire and Agna or light...off the charts!"

"The explanation for this, Yeshua, is the electrical charges stored in your body are abnormally high, similar to those of the Yoga Kriya Kundalini Yoga Masters, including Satguru Agastyar, Satguru Boganathar, Satguru Thirumoolar, Satguru Rama Devar, Satguru Konkanavar, Satguru Valmiki, among many others! I have also noticed the field of light that surrounds your body...your aura... keeps increasing and intensifying, Yeshua."

"This is surely what God wants of us if we are able to heal others" Yeshua responded. "I realize most people think sickness and disease come from sin, and in a sense, that is true, but not in the conventional way it is deemed to happen...from our transgressions against God. The concept of sin has been perverted by a collective of clerics who want to control their parishioners. Sin is nothing more than ignorance of something...not knowing better. We must ask, 'just who is not teaching the people better?' It is the clerics, so the problem is exacerbated and becomes a vicious cycle!"

"Because of this I can see in my future where I might be butting heads with the Pharisees and Sadducees, in my own land of Israel!"

"Well, Yeshua, this is clearly because of the nature of governments and religions," Thoth replied, "those who try to enlighten and liberate the masses will always be attacked by these institutions. It is primarily a power issue, but is a control issue, as well! These entities like to supplant God, because they make a living doing so, which in a great many cases is the only way they can provide for themselves. And, since they possess no other skills or abilities by which to support themselves and their families, they are more like parasites than anything of value!"

"I guess I will cross that bridge, when and if I have to, Thoth," Yeshua replied in a circumspect manner, not really wanting to contemplate the topic further. "Yet actually, when I consider your words, Thoth, I guess I have already crossed that bridge, as you well perceive. Irrespective of this, the only thing that is important is our devotion to God and dedicating our lives to him...it has nothing to do with how many times you go to temple!"

"Really, Thoth, there is no other game in town, but if you told most people this, they would complain and frown, because their shortsightedness has prevented them for seeing and perceiving such!"

Brahmin Hanuman, the leader of the Vishnu Temple in Varanasi, overheard the conversation between Yeshua and Thoth, and suggested they consider travelling to Kedarnath and Badrinath, two cities close to the headwaters of the Holy Ganges River. This seemed to make a lot of sense to the two Masters. Thoth had some previous knowledge of the Sacred Ganges and explained this to me—all about the lingams, which were river smoothed stones in the shape of a phallus. They had come to be highly prized and considered to be a direct representation of God.

Overhearing this I became extremely curious about something I considered strange, and I questioned Thoth, "Can you explain what you mean by the lingams being a direct representation of God, Thoth? I really do not see the connection!"

Showing a lot of compassion and understanding, Thoth replied, "Let me see, James, if I can get you on the right track. You see, the lingam is a representation of the phallus, which has to do with

In the Shadow of a Master

Dr. Robert J. Newton

fertility and creation and the penis and its role in the creating of new beings on Earth. Whereas in your Hebrew traditions, you dismiss pantheism...meaning God is in everything, and you will find in Hinduism and Yoga, the Lord Shiva God is seen in any and all aspects of creation. Another aspect of this is discussed in my Smgardine Tablet; it describes how the Creator formed everything in a state of non-duality— interconnectedness—which I have mentioned before!"

I raised my eyebrows and nodded my head up and down in understanding; I replied, "That makes sense to me, Thoth, even though it is not recorded, noted, nor considered in my Jewish traditions, yet maybe it should be! But another thing I am curious about is the role of a Brahmin. Do you know about that?"

Thoth, appreciating my curiosity, graciously replied, "Yes. James, I think I can speak to that issue. As you probably know, the Brahmin traditionally starts out as an aspirant...learning and studying the ancient Indian texts, including The Vedas and The Upanishads. After years of tutelage from a veteran Brahmin, the aspirant is certified to preside over a Hindu temple, and ministering to the Indian population, at large, acts as a go between for them, with Shiva, God."

A large smile came over my face, in appreciation of Thoth's explanation, as I sincerely proffered, "I am most grateful for your explanation of this, Master Thoth!"

Thoth acknowledged me, nodding his head up and down in the gentle rocking motion to which I had grown comfortable. At sunset, a meal was prepared in the Varanasi Vishnu Temple, where we all partook in the delicious meal of basmati rice, lentils, with vegetable biryani and masala sauce. The aroma of the food was so enticing, even Yeshua took notice. I had come to know he was normally not swayed by or a slave to food, but the way the odors of the food blended together this day was compelling...tantalizing!

As honored visitors, we were served first, along with Brahmin Hanaman. Instead of eating his food rapidly, Master Yeshua ate very slowly, chewing each bite of his food 108 times, which made it easier to digest, but just as important, it allowed him the added privilege to savor the appetizing fare, while eating extraordinarily little.

After dinner we thanked Brahmin Hanuman for his hospitality; Hanuman and his priests started a large fire in the middle of the temple. Surrounded by this large and hot fire, we experienced a Yagna ceremony, where all the participants repeated an extended session of mantra. Before the ceremony, everyone put a dot of verbuti on their forehead, by their third eye and pineal gland, as a mark of surrender to God. They also put their moistened fingers in holy ash from a previous Yagni ceremony, and wiped this across their forehead, parallel to the forehead lines, leaving three or four lines imprinted thereon. The purpose of this ceremonial action was to receive the purifying energy contained in the holy ash. The Yagni was considered an act of dharma—duty—to praise and live, in compliance with the laws of God.

Once the Yagni fire was well established, Brahmin Hanuman, his priests, and Yeshua, Thoth, and I were seated in a ring around the fire. The Yagni fire had some camphor wood, which was considered purifying, as well releasing a pleasing fragrance. Brahmin Hanuman began repeating the Gayatri Mantra, which was a praise of the Sun aspect of God. Then in response, the rest of the Yagni participants repeated the Gayatri Mantra, as well, in a call and response format. The power of the Gayatri was not only known and respected by Brahmin Hanuman, but by the entire populace of India.

Master Yeshua was infused with so much intense Prana...Kundalini, he became enshrouded in a ball of light—a Merkabah—and ascended into the Heavens, above. Master Thoth also became infused in an intense Kundalini energy, as well, but remained incarnate around the fire.

I quietly took in the call and response of the Gayatri Mantra. As it continued, unabated, I slowly began to review what he saw in the ascension of Yeshua and the highly energized state of kundalini, which I saw Thoth experience. As I reviewed his thoughts and recollections of all this, I thought, *this is beyond the beyond! Nary a soul in Israel knows about this, and yet what Master Yeshua just did would leave them in a state of disbelief. This is exactly what humanity needs to transcend the limitations we seem to face on Earth, so we can establish our divine right and connection to God, as per the 59th Names of God in the Torah in Exodus 14, Hey Resh Chet—with us being connected to the light. It will be interesting to see how Yeshua uses and shares this process with humanity.*

The Yagni ceremony and the call and response of the Gayatri Mantra continued for six hours. Throughout the ritual, as an offering to God the various participants threw rice and fruit and milk and ghee butter into the fire. When the ceremony was over, Master Yeshua teleported himself back to the Vishnu temple in a Merkabah, and I had innumerable questions to ask him, beginning with, "Master, where did you go and what did you experience?"

"I must admit, James, I don't believe I've experienced anything like I did, tonight. It is certainly something I need to share with our people in Israel and other places we visit," As Yeshua continued to quench my curiosity, he said, in a humble and subdued manner, "I ascended through the fourth paradise, to the fifth, and sequentially to the six, seventh, eighth, and ninth paradises, James. The Ninth Paradise is the abode of the high angels, and everything there is manifested as energy; there is not even a remote vestige of dense matter."

"Even the fourth paradise is a huge upgrade to a third-paradise Earth, where the illusion of dense matter is revealed as more energy than matter! I think I have mentioned before, and as we have uncovered, that dense matter does not exist—even though on Earth it definitely appears to be real! So, James, by meditating deeply and through the sacred mantra prayers, like Gayatri, we can bring more energy into our bodies and minds, and pierce through the illusion of matter...and that matters a lot, as it were, if we are ever to attain and claim our divine potential!"

A slight pause in his discourse, and I was moved to hear Yeshua's probing question, "Did you feel the power of the Gayatri Mantra during the Yagni ceremony we just experienced, James?"

"Yes, but tell me more about the Gayatri prayer, Rabboni?" I continued to quiz Yeshua. "I feel compelled to learn more about it!"

"Brahmin Hanuman shared with me information about this sacred Hindu prayer. As he explained, the invocation exalts and praises our Lord God, in its feminine aspect, known as Gayatri Devi, James," Yeshua replied. "It is a prayer—actually a mantra—that when repeated 108 times, continuously, gains the full force, effect, and benefit of it. This sacred refrain is known to be thousands, if not millions and maybe even billions of years old! Everyone in India knowns the Gayatri! It is easily recognized because of how it creates a highly cymatic, or vibrational effect from the Indian Sanskrit language. Through those vibrations a sacred energy is created, which is proven to manifest prosperity, wisdom, and enlightenment. It is also known to help mitigate our karma, so we can re-attain our divine connection to God, as per the 7th Name of God, Aleph Kaf Aleph, which translated to: *restoring things to their perfect state!*"

I knew my curiosity had taken a turn toward a deep probing of the topic when I continued my questioning. "What do you mean by karma, Master? Is that like evil and sin?"

"Those are most salient questions, James," Yeshua replied in a sincere effort to assuage my intense desire to understand.

"First, there is no sin—in the sense of a bad act. If it actually connotes ignorance—not knowing better—so we must first ask, 'How can that be bad?' Neither, James, is karma evil, but more clearly defined as the unfair and inequitable acts we commit against others. Acts which then diminish us until we mitigate those acts with a positive action to cancel them out! No one can do this for us, James. We must do it ourselves!"

"Wow," I declared, in a state of amazement as I found clarity. "That is so different from what we learned in our studies of the Torah and with the Essenes. However, it makes perfect sense and pleases me greatly to know because I have felt guilty about things I have done in the past and burdened by each. Yet, you, Yeshua, have shown me how to make amends with others, for which I am most grateful!"

"Put your mind at rest, James," Yeshua replied. I was touched by the assurance in his voice, and elated when he said, "We will be

In the Shadow of a Master

Dr. Robert J. Newton

doing great things together in the future! We will depart for Kedarnath in the morning, with Thoth, and continue our adventure in the Vishnu Temple there! There will be a lot of snow and ice there, so we will need to use what we learned in Tibet—when we melted frozen sheets on our bodies, to keep ourselves warm!"

CHAPTER 8

OFF TO KEDARNATH, BADRINATH, AND THE HEAD
WATERS OF THE GANGES RIVER AND MEETING AN
EXALTED YOGI.

AT FIRST LIGHT IN the morning, we began our daily meditation, combined with the Gayatri Mantra, at the Vishnu Temple in Varanasi. Yeshua let it be known this was an optimal way to begin and progress through the day. Of course, I took special notice, and when after an hour of meditation our mantra session was finished, Brahmin Hanuman had his priests bring us a breakfast to eat. Again, the food was not only filled with pleasing scents, but contained varied fruits with delicious and nourishing properties, and naan bread.

After finishing the repast, we arose and thanked Brahmin Hanuman for his hospitality, and began our trek to Kedarnath, with our lowly donkey in tow. It became progressively colder as we progressed on our trip to Kedarnath. It turned into a four-day journey even at a brisk pace. This concerned Yeshua not a bit! I smiled inside as I saw how he enjoyed meeting the people in small villages along the way. There were poignant moments finding the village people more than open to giving us lodging and food. Like I had once been, many were attracted to and amazed by the intense light and aura, which surrounded Yeshua's body. Yeshua was repeatedly referred to by his Issa and Isha names and their iterations, with great adulation and adoration bestowed upon him.

As we reached the Shiva Temple in Kedarnath, Thoth divulged, "This temple is famous for having 12 Jyotirlingas which I had come to know were considered the most sacred abodes of Shiva and came from the headwaters of the Ganges River. It is important to know the temple is considered auspicious and highly revered among the Hindu pilgrims who visit it, because these are considered lingams of light that wash away karma and purify a soul and body…believed to be extra ordinarily infused with the energy or prana of God."

Yeshua raised his eyebrows as he acknowledged the significance and usefulness of this information. Making this observation, I then questioned Thoth, asking, "Is this just myth, Thoth, or are there real benefits from being near to these twelve lingams?"

"I will answer you like this, James," Thoth replied with hint of certainty in his voice. "The many Hindu pilgrims are not here for the warm climate, which we know does not exist, but rather for the benefits of the twelve lingams that are said to be infused with the energy of Lord Shiva God! These Jyotirlinga are light and intense energy…light which is an infusion of energy from our Creator/God and can allow us to achieve more and ultimately move to the doorstep of enlightenment, which should be our primary goal in life!"

"Those insights," I responded, with a fresh, expanded mind, "have really opened my eyes, Thoth, and the wisdom you have accrued over the ages certainly serves you well!"

Meanwhile, after respectfully listening to Thoth's words, Yeshua became otherwise occupied by group of villagers in the vicinity of the Shiva Temple. The group had heard of Yeshua's healing work at the two temples in Varanasi; they flocked to the site, coming for healing of maladies and minds, clamoring for St. Issa. The Brahmin priest of this temple, Arjun, had created a line for the healing patients, and as he introduced himself to Yeshua, assured that he would control and account for the people in the line.

Yeshua responded to him in gratitude and with a wry smile on his face, told Brahmin Arjun to tell the gathering crowd that everyone would get their turn to be healed. What he did not tell Arjun was he was going to heal every person, and a few animals, simultaneously. Yeshua sat down in the lotus meditation posture, his legs crossed, with his heels tucked into each groin. The crowd watched as his body became infused with so much prana energy. It glowed like an intensely bright orb, due to his performing the Pranayam(a) meditation, and continuous recitations of the Gayatri Mantra prayer. This light did not go unnoticed by those seeking to be healed; they couldn't stop staring at him in obvious adulation. While they fully expected him to heal each of them separately. Much to the chagrin of the crowd, Yeshua took a new page from his book and announced his decision to heal all of them at once. His healing went beyond this crowd as he boldly healed everyone in a many-mile's radius of the Kedarnath Shiva Temple.

In the Shadow of a Master

Dr. Robert J. Newton

Brahmin Arjun, amazed at what he saw, approached Yeshua with great respect, and bowed before him. In a show of equal respect and honor, Yeshua bowed back and replied, "Thank you for giving me this forum to heal these people, Arjun. This will bless your temple, as well, and will be a boon and blessing for everyone who visits this holy temple!"

Upon witnessing this conversation, I was compelled to question Yeshua, in a state of astonishment, "Master Yeshua, there are people flooding in from several nearby villages outside the temple, telling Brahmin Arjun of your healing miracles! How do you accomplish simultaneous healing and the distant healing as well? Can you teach me to do this?"

"The key lies in the Pranayam(a) meditation, which we recently learned, and the Djed meditation we learned from Thoth while in Egypt, James," Yeshua confidently replied, in a tone clearly meant to assure me. "You can, in fact, do anything I do, but you must be more dedicated to an assiduous practice of the Pranayam(a) extended breathing meditation, in conjunction with the Gayatri mantra/prayer."

Yeshua shifted from serious contemplation, to a fun spirit he knew I would enjoy, saying, "The more you do, the better your stew. The more you know, the further you go! On a more serious note, however, James, engaging in an assiduous dedication of practicing Pranayam(a) will serve you well when we meet with Satguru Agastyar, as Satguru Boganathar foretold us we would!"

"Yes, Master Yeshua—my Rabboni—it is impossible to disagree with the logic and wisdom of your words and guidance." As I replied, my heart and throat constricted with an intense gratitude. It was visible in my voice and hand gestures as I spoke, "I

70

definitely have to up my game to match my dedication to such a practice!"

Almost as an effort to put me at ease, Thoth chose that moment to interject his observations of the huge group healing Yeshua performed. "Your fame, Yeshua, has traveled far and wide in India, as it did in Tibet and Nepal. This is warranted and deserved as by the works we perform, rather than by our words...words which can come easily and too often soon forgotten, as we establish our value to humanity!"

"It is possible our work is done here, and we should proceed to Badrinath. I am told there exists a Lord Vishnu temple, with a statue of Lord Badrinarayan, devotee of Vishnu, which is considered among the most important Hindu temples in India. While it is about a thousand feet lower than the Kedarnath Shiva Temple— at more than 11,000 feet—it still will be cold there, with plenteous snow. Despite the cold, Hindu legend says a pilgrim can overcome their moksha—reincarnation— the cycle of life and death, by visiting this temple! This temple is one of the four sacred Hindu temples here, which Lord Vishnu incarnated on Earth. We know this temple is about 1500 years old and Hindu pilgrims have been coming here for the duration. Many people travel thousands of miles to visit this temple, as well as the Kedarnath Temple. That alone tells us something special is going on there!"

Most grateful for the things shared by Thoth, Yeshua proclaimed, "It is impossible for me to disagree with your narrative, Thoth, and that alone would compel us to make a trip thereto."

Being most grateful for, and amazed about, what Yeshua had attained in the wide scale healing event, following a short discussion, Brahmin Arjun brought food for the three pilgrims to consume. Although neither Yeshua or Thoth were hungry or really in need of food, the savory scents of curry, ginger, cardamom spices in the food was so tantalizing, they could not resist eating, and were equally grateful for Arjun's gesture.

After dinner, and a discussion with Brahmin Arjun about the finer points of healing the body and mind, of which it was growing obvious Yeshua was becoming a Master, sleep time approached. This time, I decided to spend more time engaging in the pranayama extended breathing meditation and the Gayatri Mantra, and devoting less time to sleeping, just as I had been urged to do by Yeshua.

As usual, Yeshua and Thoth meditated through the night, while repeating the Gayatri Mantra. When the sun broke through the mountains in the morning, Yeshua was anxious to depart on the trip to Badrinath. I finished my morning session of Pranayam(a) and Gayatri Mantra, and we sought out Brahmin Arjun to thank him for his hospitality and the sumptuous food. Arjun would not let us leave, however, until we had consumed some rice, lentils and the naan bread his priests had prepared for us. Being gracious and wanting to foster good will with Brahmin Arjun, we consumed the delicious food, and then were off to Badrinath, followed, of course, by our trusty donkey.

Moving along the snow-covered road to Badrinath, we soon looked like a parade...the people from the small villages between Kedarnath and Badrinath lined the road and praised, clapped, and shouted Yeshua's Indian names, St. Issa and Isha Mishai. It was hard for them to contain their excitement, since so many people had been healed in Yeshua's mass-healing ceremony.

In the Shadow of a Master

Dr. Robert J. Newton

Although Yeshua was in no need of adulation in any way, shape, or form, since he knew all healing came from the power and energy of God and no place else, I sensed it must have been nice to be appreciated by the masses, nevertheless. Many women brought their babies to be blessed by Yeshua, and he obliged. I observed his body language, which reflected he was naturally attracted to the innocence of babies and young children; he appeared to be literally compelled to be around them. It was instinctual for him to bless them, as was his connection to God, most right and tight.

Thoth, being a great Master himself, was in no way insulted that he was not getting the same attention as Yeshua. He, too, was amazed by what Yeshua had performed during their trip; he also sensed just how big a splash Yeshua would make...what an impact he would make when he eventually returned to Israel. On a hunch, I started repeating the Gayatri Mantra, aloud, and the people joined in with me, as did Thoth and Yeshua.

Brahmin Arjun had decided to try and join our caravan, and he did eventually catch up to us with a donkey pulling a cart he rode. Arjun shared just how glad he was to have made this decision because his intuition told him something incredibly special would happen when Yeshua passed through the small villages. He also brought with him a copy of the *Bhagavad Gita*, which he gifted to Yeshua. This had information and instruction from Lord Krishna, an Indian son of God...Lord Vishnu... and who also came to fight the forces of evil in India, who were known as mlecchas/barbarians!

Moved by Arjun's gift, Yeshua embraced him with an extended hug. I stood with mouth agape as the Yeshua and the Brahmin both began to glow; an intense light surrounded their bodies and head. The glow did not escape the notice of the villagers following Yeshua.

These humble farmers, craftspeople, shopkeepers, and their families all knew they were in the presence of a Master, as they viewed the amazing things done by Yeshua.

Yeshua could feel the intense energy in the Lord Vishnu temple in Badrinath from many miles away, being generated by Lord Vishnu, part of the triad of God, including Lord Shiva and Lord Brahma. Thoth noticed the energy as well and motioned to Yeshua as he pointed to the road ahead and moved the fingers on each hand, shifting them back into his chest. Yeshua smiled and nodded his head up and down, in agreement about the intense energy from Vishnu.

Because the trip to Badrinath was a long two-day journey, one of the villagers along the way, begged for us, and more specifically, Yeshua, to lodge with them for the night. I was most grateful for the offer of hospitality, because sleeping outside, at night, was very cold, and certainly Yeshua and Thoth and Brahmin Arjun, were, as well.

When we entered the home of Deepak, which was actually a hut, Yeshua noticed they did not have an inside heater, so he manifested one into existence. It seemed a small task to focus his mind on creating one and then using a burst of prana to bring it into existence. Overjoyed, Deepak's wife, Sita, bowed before Yeshua and kissed his feet, in respect and appreciation, repeatedly voicing, blessed be St. Isha Masiha. She knew her children would be vastly more comfortable during the cold nights the family generally experienced at an elevation of 10,000 feet. It was with a deep sense of gratitude that Sita went outside and began to prepare the nightly meal. However, when she got outside, Sita was surprised and overjoyed to see a large pile of vegetables and fruits, from which to create a meal, all of which had been manifested by Yeshua.

In the Shadow of a Master

Dr. Robert J. Newton

Sita put her heart into creating a meal for the great Master who had entered their humble abode. She took rice and lentils and mixed them with carrots, beets, broccoli, onions, and garlic—and infused them with spices of curry, ginger, cinnamon and cardamon. When the food was ready for consumption, she brought it into the house and served Yeshua and Thoth, first, then James and her husband, followed by her children.

Deepak gave thanks for their bounty of food, as he repeated the Gayatri Mantra and blessed St. Issa Mishiya. Everyone enjoyed the sumptuous fare, savoring each bite. For dessert, Sita served sliced pieces of mango, cherimoya, and jack fruit, rarely found, or eaten in the foothills of the Himalayas, between Kedarnath and Badrinath. Deepak put a few pieces of wood in the new heater which had been manifested from the ethers by Yeshua. The entire family was euphoric about the stove and could not believe their good fortune. My heart felt their joy as they continued to thank Yeshua for his gift to them.

As they slept in the crowded hut, Thoth and Yeshua and James and Arjun engaged in their rituals of pranayama(a) extended breathing meditation and concurrent recitation of the Gayatri Mantra, which was equivalent to sleep, and a superior substitute for such. The energy they created in the Pranayam(a) created enough heat to keep them warm throughout the cold mountain night temperatures, irrespective of the heater.

The more I practiced the rituals, the more I was remotely able to replicate the feats of Yeshua and Thoth, in small measure. Brahmin Arjun and I were able to do the pranayama(a) meditation in conjunction with the Gayatri Mantra for half the night before we dozed off into a deep sleep.

In the Shadow of a Master

Dr. Robert J. Newton

Being outside the hut, as the sun peaked through the mountains, Arjun and I awakened to Yeshua and Thoth still meditating. When they sensed we were awake, they both looked over at us, smiling, nodding their heads up and down. I knew from previously experiencing that nodding motion they were impressed that we had spent half the night in meditation. Sita was also up at first light as well; we found her preparing a breakfast of rice, kidney beans, broccoli, and naan bread, as well as slices of Mango, for her family and to honor her guests.

Appreciative of Sita's efforts, Yeshua looked over at her, smiling, and remarked, "I sense your devotion to your family, and it brings a good feeling to my heart."

"Namaste, namaskar," Sita remarked, most appreciative of Yeshua acknowledging her familial devotion. "Please get a plate and I will feed all of your party. I am so appreciative for the food you manifested for us yesterday…and for our heater."

Yeshua put his hands together, extended, as in prayer, and bowed to Sita. This brought a wide smile to her face, and she focused again on feeding her guests, particularly since the tantalizing odors of the food made it hard to resist. After we finished our food, we thanked Deepak and Sita for their hospitality. Brahmin Arjun suggested we get in his cart and tie our donkey to the back of it. Grateful, we gratefully accepted his offer, and headed toward Badrinath.

While in route, Thoth mentioned once again the importance of the twelve lingams, and stimulated Yeshua' s interest in them. Throughout their journey to Shiva Temple Badrinath, he quizzed Brahmin Arjun about the properties and application of these large stones of basalt rock. Arjun explained, "These stones have been

76

In the Shadow of a Master

Dr. Robert J. Newton

smoothed in the headwater of the River Ganges, just below the Gangotri Glacier. They also are comprised of almost half silicon dioxide, which is what most people call quartz, and it is infused with a special electrical potential, from the Creator, Shiva, itself. Because of this, many pilgrims from all over India come here—seemingly compelled—as there are many stories of people being able to eliminate their bad karma...their moksha...by mediating inside the temple, in conjunction with getting blessings and prayers from the Hindu monks, in the temple. Along with my Kedarnath Temple, this is another of those four auspicious Hindu temples in India."

"I was starting to sense and intuit much of what you shared, Arjun," Yeshua noted with appreciation in his voice. "And I guess the auspiciousness of the temple has do with its proximate location to the headwaters of the River Ganges, right Arjun?"

"Indeed," Arjun replied with a hint of authority in his voice. "The source of any river is its most intense point of power, and the Ganges is considered the life blood and soul of the Indian nation. Since our country is thousands—if not millions—of years old, our traditions about this run deep and everyone understands and takes advantage of such, whenever they can. There are always pilgrims— seekers of God—coming to Kedarnath and Badrinath."

"Yes. Yes. This makes sense, Arjun," Yeshua replied in a confirming voice. "Since we have our Temple Mount in Jerusalem, a place where pilgrim s come to worship, as well, James and I visited there, once, right, James?"

"Yes, indeed, Master," I concurred. "And it is most interesting what Brahmin Arjun has shared with us, as well as useful! I guess he would know more about his Shiva Temple in Kedarnath than anyone else!"

77

In the Shadow of a Master

Dr. Robert J. Newton

Arjun then suggested, "I am sure if you go to the headwaters of the Ganges, you will find Satguru Agastyar—who is known as the immortal guru—can instruct the three of you in the finer points and higher aspects of Kriya Kundalini. He is very picky about whom he entertains and takes an audience with. He is the one who initiated Satguru Boganathar into the breathless state of immortality, known as Soruba Samadhi. This is a state which allows us to circumvent the sting of death and to move about in a ball of light, to teleport ourselves, and discern the past, present and the future by pulling knowledge from the skies—a practice known as akashic knowledge."

Hoping my voice displayed the authority I hoped to portray, I declared, "Master Yeshua already knows how to travel within the light, Arjun, but he has always open to learning more. Right Master?"

"I agree, James," Yeshua nodded his head up and down, with the now expected gentle, sublime smile on his face, "that is the operating system on Earth, which is constant learning and evolution. Since God, itself, is evolving and learning, so must we, lest we be left forever behind!"

"Going to the headwaters seems like a plan," Thoth replied with a voice reflecting his assent, "it will be most interesting to have an audience with Satguru Agastyar and learn from his wisdom and knowledge. Why don't we make our trek there in the morning...at first light!"

Yeshua and I nodded to show our agreement, but in the meantime, we noticed every one of our party was already engaged in Kriya Kundalini Pranayam, practicing extended breathing meditation as they completed what appeared to be hundreds of recitations of the Gayatri Mantra prayer. Yeshua suggested we fast so as to allow our bodies to be more infused with prana/light, since digesting food impairs that process. Everyone agreed and created a little magic—actually a lot of it—and dozed off to sleep in the wee hours of the late night.

In the Shadow of a Master

Dr. Robert J. Newton

CHAPTER 9

FEELING THE ALLURE OF THE HEADWATERS OF THE RIVER GANGES AND THE GANGOTRI GLACIER.

AS THE SUN AROSE in the morning, we were wrapped in the warmth of pink, orange, and yellow hues in the sky. We left, after thanking Brahmin Hanuman and began our journey transported in Arjun's donkey cart with Brahmin Arjun. We traveled the road to the headwaters, near the Gangotri Glacier, but this time, we also hitched our donkey to the cart because the road was steep, and the load was heavy with the weight of many bodies. Actually, Yeshua and Thoth could have light traveled in a second or two to the glacier but moving at that speed made sightseeing virtually impossible. There were also other pilgrims along the road to the Ganges headwaters, to receive blessings from the Holy Ganges River in their lives.

One such pilgrim—the venerated Kriya Kundalini Yoga Avatar, Agastyar—was on the trail with Kriya Kundalini Yoga Avatar,

In the Shadow of a Master

Dr. Robert J. Newton

Boganathar (Bogar). Since they were walking and Yeshua and the rest of us were settled in the donkey cart, we caught up to Agastyar and Boganathar, along the road. As soon as he spotted us, Boganathur greeted us with the traditional Indian greeting, *Namaste*, and clasped his hands over his heart. Yeshua replied in kind and clasped his hands over his heart and replied with *Shalom*, the traditional Jewish greeting. Thoth replied with *praise be to God Ra* as he clasped his hands over his heart. Each greeting was genuine and heart-felt; Yeshua's extended beyond, to mean, *what I have done for you is because of the Blessings of God and nothing of my ability or contribution.*

Before I could greet Boganathur, he welcomed me and shared his observation, "I see you have been practicing your Kriya Kundalini Pranayam(a) and Gayatri Mantra; I trust you are aware that the light around your body has expanded, considerably!"

I felt honored and could only hope my words truly expressed my appreciation. "I must thank you, Master Boganathar for your observation and tutelage. Many amazing things have happened since we met you in the mountain pass on the way to Varanasi. I sense you are accompanied by your Master, Agastyar, right?"

"You would be correct on that account, and as I remember, you wanted to learn to heal like Master Yeshua and I declared you would learn this from Master Agastyar later in your trip, and so now you are both here—do you not find that auspicious!" Boganathar exclaimed, in an exaggerated manner, all the while, smiling, and releasing a hearty laugh. "So, James, let me now introduce you to Kriya Kundalini Yoga Avatar, Satguru Agastyar."

After a minute or two, searching for the proper words to address Agastyar, I announced, "We know nothing of you in Israel,

82

but I know you are held in great esteem in India, Satguru Agastyar, and I would be blessed to have you share your knowledge of healing with me, as well as anything else you might so generously reveal."

"Thank you for acknowledging me, James, and because you have been initiated into Kriya Kundalini Yoga, as have Masters Yeshua and Thoth, I will give all of you an advanced class on healing when we arrive at the headwaters of the Ganges River in Gangotri. Perhaps I might be able to learn about healing from Master Yeshua, myself! We should be in Gangotri about midafternoon. We can find lodging in a cave nearby and then we shall begin the healing class.

Along the road to Gangotri, I was fascinated to hear Boganathar, Agastyar, Yeshua, and Thoth discuss, among them, exactly how a healing occurs. Yeshua and Thoth and I decided to disembark from the donkey cart, to ensure our conversation could be more intimate. Yeshua was discussing different names from *the 72 Names of God*, in Exodus 14:19-21 of the Torah, as a means to effectuate healing, including the 5th Name of God, Mem Hey Shin (healing), Hey Resh Chet (connected to the light), and Aleph Kaf Aleph (Restoring things to their perfect state), and how he had healed myriad people and even a donkey with this protocol.

I listened intently as Master Thoth discussed *the Papyrus Ani* and invoking Sekhmet and Anubis to take a body into a state of immortality—obviating the need to die. Boganathar and Agastyar discussed the concept of Intelligent Cosmic Vibration, consisting of Yagna/fire, Agna/light, and Aum, the cosmic sound of creation—and using these to heal and regenerate bodies and transit them to a state of immortality. Moments seemed like hours as Agastyar referred to Satguru Patanjali's *The Yoga Sutras*, and how practicing Kriya Kundalini Dhyana and Kriya Kundalini Pranayam(a), would lift a body into a state of Soruba Samadhi...a condition of perfect health and immortality.

They conversed; I sucked it all in like a dry sponge, and realizing I was surrounded by highly evolved and uplifted, wisemen...wise souls. We were approaching a huge glacier, and a raging river, which I assumed to be the Gangotri Glacier and the headwater of the Holy River Ganges. Satgurus Agastyar and Boganathar confirmed my hunches and started talking about the headwaters and the Gangotri Glacier, which bountifully supplies the Ganges with water. They also mentioned how this glaciated water was not only holy, but healing, as well. It contains more hydrogen and oxygen than other water sources, and a vastly higher mineral content. I caught a glance at Agastyar looking my direction to make sure I heard his comments about the healing properties of the water. He also mentioned how said water could aid one to achieve the state of Soruba Samadhi and transcend the ravages of death.

I had the distinct feeling that although Yeshua had successfully healed people on this journey, he was equally attentive to Agastya's narrative. Shortly after, Yeshua mentioned his gratitude for the knowledge being shared and I could tell what Yeshua was learning had set his mind in motion and he was attempting to integrate what he learned into what he already knew.

Looking back on those conversations, I knew, for me, this was the zenith of our journey to faraway lands, and it seemed to me the same was true for Yeshua. Agastyar explained how glaciated water and the water in fast moving streams had more atoms of hydrogen and oxygen than domestic water supplies and provides a body more energy and the possibility to create an energy source different from food or calories—glycolic phosphorylation—and subsequently replace it with oxidative phosphorylation, which occurs through oxygen, hydrogen, and carbon in conjunction with sunlight and/or the extended breath achieved through Kriya Kundalini pranayama(a), which infused more oxygen and hydrogen into a body, helping to catalyze a state of an immortalized body.

I was overwhelmed by this information at first, just due to it being very foreign to me, yet unlike me Yeshua and Thoth understood and accepted this immediately. Additionally, Master Yeshua manifested a large tent for us to sleep in, instead of sleeping in a cave, with the requisite attendants to erect such. Really, this was more for me than the other four men I was surrounded with... all living legends...wise and knowledgeable souls living in a state of immortality...each very intricately connected to God.

My mind all astir, I started a fire in the middle of the large tent, situated next to the headwaters of the Ganges. My intention for the fire was for cooking and warmth, but both Satguru Agastyar and Boganathar decided we need to have a Yagna/fire ceremony; each promising me it would be something I would never forget. Of course, not being one to miss something great, I attempted to gather a lot of firewood for the seven-hour fire ceremony, which was quite a task since right at the tree line where we were situated there were not many trees or dead wood. I need not have been concerned...Master Yeshua quickly manifested a cord of wood from the ethers. Agastyar asked me to get the fire stoked with wood, and create a large fire, which I was glad to do.

Once the flames of the fire had peaked, Agastyar gathered everyone together for the Yagna ceremony. Once we were circled around the fire pit, Agastyar recited the Mahamrityunjaya

Mantra/Prayer, which was followed by the rest of us responding with our repetition of this mantra. For seven hours the evening was alive with a continual call and response.

Agastyar and Boganathar explained to me that the purpose of the Yagna/fire is a process of self-purification and supplication to God, and that during this process it is possible to uplift one's consciousness into the higher Dimensions and levels of Heaven. I can sincerely report that as I began to be pulled into the energy/prana of the fire, I felt myself getting lighter and being pulled literally upward into the higher Dimensions, wherein Heaven exists. My inner guidance, conveyed to me when I had reached was the fourth Dimension, where I found the emotion overwhelming! I found it difficult to describe the feeling of being liberated from the bonds and limitations of Earth.

While on this particular sojourn I also met and conversed with many of my relatives and ancestors, who had died and lived in this fourth Dimension, which I found was called the Fourth Paradise of Heaven. It took little time to realize I was much happier here than anywhere or anything I experienced on Earth. In this cognitive moment I thought to myself, *I've enjoyed being able to think about something and having it manifested into existence—this is probably much like Master Yeshua routinely attains.*

After some time in the Fourth Paradise—and I am not really sure how long I was there because time had little meaning or reference for where I was—I felt myself getting lifted into an even higher Dimension. My inner knowingness led me to understand this was the Fifth Dimension, known also as the Fifth Paradise of Heaven. As much as the energy in the Fourth Dimension was an upgrade to that on Earth, I now felt the same comparison of available energy between the Fifth and the Fourth Paradises (Dimensions). There was exceedingly more vitality, which some would call spirit, in which to manifest whatever I needed...be it an object or food or being in a certain place in the wink of an eye. I also started detecting the presence of angels and embraced the great comfort I found in being surrounded by these emissaries from God.

Somehow, Master Yeshua mentally tied into where I was and gently whispered in my ear, "Why don't you attempt to ascend to the Ninth Paradise... the Ninth Dimension...where many high angels reside? It should be simple for you now. You just take your breathing cadence and extend it as much as possible, as in the Kriya Kundalini Pranayam(a)extended breath."

Without speaking, I looked up at my Rabboni and nodded my head and up and down with the now familiar gesture to signify agreement and appreciation. What followed was more than an experience! While Agastyar would complete his round of the mantra, I would take in my breath, and on the call and response, with my eyes, but not my head, turned upward...I would let my breath out very slowly. Boganathar had taught how this process of the upturned eye was a reliable way to pull oneself into the higher Dimensions.

Before long, I felt myself being pulled into the Ninth Paradise, where I conversed with different angels, including Anchaiah, the 7th Angel of God, commensurate with the 7th Name of God, Aleph Kaf Aleph, which means to restore things to their perfect state. I asked Anchaiah about my experience and he mentally responded, *I am the angel of learning and wisdom, and these things are necessary to restore things to their perfect state, as the Creator originally manifested things!*

In the Shadow of a Master

Dr. Robert J. Newton

I was grateful, beyond any and all measures, for Anchaiah' s words, which confirmed what Yeshua and I learned in the Essense temple; they validated what we had previously learned, which really made my night—I let the fire pull me and keep me in the higher Dimensions, where a deeper spirituality and love encircled me.

When the Yagna ceremony ended, following seven long hours of call and response of the Mahamrityunjaya Mantra/Prayer, I knew my life had been very enriched that night. I found a new reality... a better understanding of the higher Dimensions and the more intense love therein. I would better understand and appreciate the things Yeshua shared with me and the things I witnessed him performing and manifesting.

When I questioned Yeshua about his experience of the Yagna fire ceremony, he replied with even more confidence than he normally exuded, as he said, "First, I want to congratulate you for the deep spiritual infusion of knowledge and abilities you just experienced, by the higher Dimensions and realms into which you pulled yourself! This just confirms my hunches about you were, correct, James, and I'd not want to further experience this trip without your special presence"

"For myself, I experienced an extended audience with Arch Angel Metatron, where I asked him many questions about the book of Enoch, which never made it into the Torah, but which we studied with the Essenes. That is why I suggested you pull yourself into the Ninth Paradise/Dimension—I was confident you had already experienced the Fifth Dimension."

I listened intently as Yeshua continued, "Metatron, who was Enoch, before his ascension into the Heavens, mentioned to me the

Dr. Robert J. Newton

Arch Angel Michael, anointed him with olive oil, to aid his ascension into from the Third Dimension on Earth, into the Fourth Paradise, and successively to the Fifth, Sixth, Seventh, Eighth, and Ninth Paradise (Dimensions)of the high angels—which in linguistic arithmetic of Hebrew Gematria of 447, reveals a God pattern and Saints of God."

"He shared that Michael then took him to the Tenth Paradise, where we have a linguistic arithmetic in Hebrew Gematria of 503— Son of the Lord and Daybreak. We also know this Tenth Dimension is where the angels of the Tree of Life, reside, including Arch Angels Michael and Metatron. This advanced learning, James, was a deep joy for me to experience."

One last thought seemed to be lingering on Yeshua's mind as he noted to me, "You should know, James, that Master Thoth experienced a journey back to his original home, in the Land of Seth, deep in the Milky Way Galaxy, where we both came from."

With all we experienced that day and evening, I thought, *Wow! This is as good as things can get.* I bowed my head and before I drifted off to sleep, I instinctively knew Yeshua had one more thing for us to experience added to his itinerary for the morrow.

In the Shadow of a Master

Dr. Robert J. Newton

CHAPTER 10

A SCALING OF THE MIGHTY MT. MERU AND LIVING IN AN ICE CAVE.

I AWOKE IN THE morning to the smell of porridge cooking over a fire. Yeshua, Thoth, Agastyar and Boganathar were deeply immersed in meditation, so I joined them, even though somewhat late to the game. It was interesting to hear their breathing so beautifully synchronized, in the extended breathing regimen of Kriya Kundalini Pranayam(a). I perceived it to be an inhale at a count of twenty and an exhale of count of forty. This long cycle of breathing, Avatar Boganathar explained to me, Yeshua, and Thoth, allowed one to access all information on Earth or elsewhere, known as the Akashic Records, which meant knowledge from the skies.

As Boganathar explained it to us, all knowledge and events were stored in a field of energy, which permeated and surrounded everything made up of extremely small particles, which were from Shiva/God, itself. If someone wanted to know about something or an event on Earth, the Milky Way Galaxy, or elsewhere, their energy needed to be focused on that—and that alone—and the information would be revealed to them. Mulling over what was being taught, I sensed Yeshua did this, without understanding the technical details of how it occurred. In fact, in my observations, he seemed to know about anything and everything—at will.

After we were finished meditating, Satguru Agastyar, who seemed to sense my thoughts, shared with me, "In fact, James, you are correct about Master Yeshua and his ability to know anything and everything, accessing the Akashic Records. You should be interested to know that you, too, have the ability to do the same— and the more and longer you engage in Kriya Kundalini Pranayam, the more you will cultivate this ability, which I can tell by looking at your aura, you have been performing in large amounts!"

"Thank you Satguru," I replied. "I recall how Satguru Bogar once remarked how you could be prickly and difficult at times, and yet my experiences with you has been anything but that!

Satguru Agastyar summoned a hearty laugh, and replied, "I do not suffer well fools and those who are not dedicated to excellence. However, your Master Yeshua is, as are you, so I was enticed to share with you the knowledge I have acquired over thousands and millions of years. As you and Yeshua learned, the Rabbi's and the Pharisees in your land have limited desire to see, learn, and transcend beyond the orthodox thoughts and ideas in which they have previously been instructed. When I was talking to Yeshua, he told me about his criticism of the Rabbi's and Pharisee's, and how they were walled-in by their beliefs—they simply don't want to see what is on the other side of those walls. So, you are blessed beyond all measure to have him as your teacher... your Satguru. Yeshua is definitely a messiah for your people—not to save them from their sins, which is just ignorance and not knowing better—but to show them they do not have to suffer the sting of death or the harness of evil!"

Continuing...and obviously deeply immersed in his message, Satguru Agastyar suddenly exclaimed, "Rama and Krishna, were our misaya's (Messiah's}, here in India! They showed us how to transcend the ravages of death and how to overcome all obstacles. They were both sons of the Lord Vishnu God. They fought the forces of evil and ignorance in epic battles, and helped lift us to our divine heritage, as God intended and in fact created for us!"

"Thank you. Namaste for sharing your knowledge and wisdom with me, Satguru Agastyar," I exclaimed as I embraced how astounded I was—and just how grateful I was for what I learned. "I will be forever in your debt!"

I glanced over and noticed how busy Yeshua was— preparing for our ascent of Mt. Meru. He put together Sherpa porters to carry our supplies up the mountain and guide us through what was reputed to be an extremely dangerous trail at the upper elevations, full of hidden cervices, hundreds of feet deep, from which very few if any, mountain climbers were saved. I could only imagine the severity of a crevice fall...resulting in broken bones...heads and a severe loss of blood or even the lack of enough rope to extricate an unfortunate victim.

Satguru Agastyar and I walked over to where Master Yeshua was coordinating our expedition and I heard Agastyar question him, "So you are still keen on an ascent of Meru, are you?"

In the Shadow of a Master

Dr. Robert J. Newton

"More than just as ascent!" Yeshua laughed aloud in response, saying, "after we summit, we will be staying up there for many months, if not longer. James is now well prepared for this, based on his experiences in our world tour and from what you and Satguru Bogar have taught him and me. I will be aided by being in the blessed state of Soruba Samadhi, up in the rare air, and who knows, James may as well! Who knows? We might be blessed to meet some Yeti's there, as well!"

Since Master Yeshua ascertained we were ready for our ascent of Mt Everest, we made provisions for our donkey to be cared for through Brahmin priest, Arjun, by the subordinate priests at his Hindu temple.

As we started to move forward on the next leg of our trek, Satguru Agastyar proclaimed, "May the energies and force of Lord Ganesha be with you on your journey! And may the Lord Lakshmi guide and make your journey safe." Yeshua and I bowed our heads in gratitude for the blessings given. Previously, we had both learned that Ganesha and Lakshmi helped remove obstacles people may encounter in their lives.

Master Thoth decided it was time for him to return to Egypt. It was clear he was not enthralled by the idea of living in perpetual, subzero temperatures and preferred the climes of Egypt's desert. So, we both bid him adieu and thanked him many times over for guiding us to myriad places and sharing his vast wealth of knowledge with us.

"May we meet again, in the land of Seth," Master Thoth exclaimed. "May the spirit of the Lord guide you and lead your way! I will send Anubis and Sekmet guide you through the underworld and protect you, wherever!"

In the Shadow of a Master

Dr. Robert J. Newton

Yeshua and I both bowed in gratitude and a state of reverence. I noticed in that moment a back-drop of huge granite and basalt boulders, and nary a tree in sight—just a raging river and massive mountains standing sentinel on the nearby horizon.

Yeshua signaled for the Sherpas to begin leading our small expedition; as they moved forward, we followed, in kind. I noticed that by the changing colors of sundown we had travelled more than two thousand feet in elevation. We had started at 12,770 feet at the foot of the Gangotri Glacier and were now at an elevation of about 15,000 feet. The more we ascended, the more belabored was my breathing and the more difficult it was to walk, and I found that engaging in Kriya Kundalini extended breath meditation made things much easier. This was superfluous for Yeshua as he was in the breathless state of Soruba Samadhi. The Sherpas set up tents and bedrolls for everyone, and one of them broke out a meal of dried fruit for us. I sadly noticed there were none of the dates we normally enjoyed.

Yeshua suggested we turn in early for sleep because he wanted to get an early start around sunrise the next morning. That sounded like a good plan to me, so I joined Yeshua and we performed more Kriya Kundalini Yoga extended breathing meditation, in conjunction with the Gayatri Mantra/prayer. Then we laid down on our bedrolls, but instead of sleeping, Yeshua practiced a Yoga Nidra meditation, which requires one to enter a rather unique state between sleep and being awake. The trick is to stay awake, as it is natural to drift off into sleep, which always happened when I tried it. However, Yeshua was a Master of this practice, because Satguru Boganathur instructed him on how achieve this state—with certain success.

95

In the Shadow of a Master

Dr. Robert J. Newton

The morning came too soon! Considering there was a blizzard outside I was noticeably concerned that it was too dangerous for us to climb Meru this day. However, Yeshua must have sensed my thoughts as he looked over at me in the tent and proclaimed, "Things will be ok... there will be good weather for us!"

I wondered how he would keep his promise, because the conditions outside tent were a cold whiteout. Yet, within a minute or so, the storm had completely abated, and it was sunny outside...not warm but no longer a freezing blizzard. I looked over at Yeshua, smiling and exclaimed, "I should have never doubted you Master. You always do what you say, and you always say what you'll do!"

Master Yeshua then looked over at me with raised eyebrows and a huge, closed mouth smile on his face. It was impossible to miss the light streaming around him... in almost blinding amounts. "I guess we can eat some dried fruit and hit the trail...no? I will notify the Sherpas!"

As we started up the trail to an anticipated 18,000 feet, Yeshua reminded me, "Remember to breathe using the pranayama(a) method. The oxygen quotient here is extremely low; retaining the breath as long as possible, will help energize your body with more oxygen and prana/energy, and you'll feel the blood pull through your body!"

I looked over at my Rabboni, trusting my glance reflected my assurance in him. I lifted my eyes upward, while looking forward— and with defined lines wrinkling my forehead. Together with Yeshua's advice and oodles of newly-formed confidence I found the trek much easier than anticipated. Neither of us knew we would encounter an icefall, full of crevices, although we were told it existed.

Later in the day, as we neared the icefall/crevices, we had to avoid them by taking an even harder route to get to our base camp, just beyond.

Yeshua could sense my trepidation, at having to scale vertical cliffs. He looked over at me and confidently declared, "Just repeat the 23rd Psalm, James. *The Lord is my shepherd, I shall not want... surely we shall dwell in the house of the lord, forever.*"

Immediately, I knew Yeshua and followed his direction... he was right...he always was! I reminded myself that he always solved the hardest problems with aplomb...he always summoned the right words for the occasion. This would serve him well, later, when we returned to Israel and he would have to deal with the discontented Rabbi's and Pharisee's, who would take issue with the correct and accurate teachings of the Lord he was destined to dispense.

In the end, I summoned the courage to scale the vertical cliffs free climbing, knowing I was now and would always be inextricably connected to our Lord God. Yeshua had so inspired me I wondered why I had been making such a big deal about this dangerous ascent. Before I knew it, we were past the icefall and its crevices through our circuitous route and arrived at the 18,000-foot base camp, with our Sherpas. Yeshua was quick to tell our Sherpas we wanted to proceed in the morning to the summit of Meru.

Astonished by Yeshua's words, the head Sherpa, Tenga, replied, "That is complete insanity...you must have a death wish, Master Yeshua! You need to acclimate to this altitude for month at the very, very least! If you do otherwise, I can confidently declare, you'll get extremely sick with uncontrollable vomiting, and most likely die a painful death. Meru is most certainly the most insane mountain to try to summit. No one has and I fear you will not either"

In the Shadow of a Master

Dr. Robert J. Newton

Yeshua looked over at Tenga, with equal confidence and replied, "I understand your concern for our welfare and realize my request is unconventional. Please rest assured we have been initiated in Kriya Kundalini Yoga by both Satguru Boganathar and Satguru Agastyar! Have you heard of them?

Tenga was in a state of astonishment, which I could see was coupled with great respect as he replied, "You studied under their tutelage? Everyone around here holds them in the highest of respect and reverence. We have seen them disappear in a ball of light. Can you do that?"

That playful side of Master Yeshua, which I had grown to value, was quite visible in the huge smile on his face and the vociferous laugh, which accompanied his reply to Tenga. Yeshua extended his arms toward Tenga, pretending to hold a ball of light in his hands, "Not only can we disappear in a ball of light, but we can also travel anywhere in a ball of light—like up to the top of that mountain, above us, in the blink of an eye!"

"That is impressive, Master Yeshua, we are already acclimated to the thin atmosphere up here. We smoke a lot of Cannabis—it makes us feel better during the arduous climb as we carry sixty to ninety-pound packs on our backs. The anandamide in the THC of the Cannabis helps us retain better moods and attitudes following these grueling climbs—and the CBD in the Cannabis help mitigate the pain in our muscles and joints."

"James and I were commenting about the acrid leaf you were smoking, Tenga. We do not have that in our homeland. We find the extended breathing meditation of Kriya Kundalini Pranayam(a), into which we have been initiated, makes us feel better when we encounter a hard task, and the hydrogen and oxygen we take into our bodies in huge amounts, helps sooth our muscles and joints. If you are interested, when we descend the mountain, which may not be for many months—if not year—I will ask Satguru Boganathar if he will initiate you into the practice, which I am quite certain he will.

Tenga smiled, something he rarely did, and nodded his head up and down and clasped his fists to Yeshua, in a state of thanks. Yeshua insisted we spend the night doing the Pranayam(a) meditation in conjunction with the Gayatri Mantra/prayer...the exaltation of the Sun aspect of the Lord God, from whence comes light and love. I experienced a wonderful, blissful state of elevated consciousness, as we continued through the night, with Master Yeshua leading the meditation. Beyond the experience, I knew it would also prepare us for a feat Yeshua had in mind...one which no one had ever before attempted, as Mt. Meru was considered too difficult and dangerous to ascend. It had never been attempted! I mulled all this over in my mind and thought, *I will be witness to this! And as well as his legendary healing, this accomplishment will most assuredly seal his legend as St. Issa Mishiya in India, Nepal, and Tibet.*

When the morning came, Yeshua told Tenga, "Just take the day off. James and I will summit Meru today and will be back in time for dinner!"

However, Tenga was concerned about their well- being, and replied with anxiety reflected in his voice, "It is bad enough to make the ascent without stopping at Base Camp, but Yeshua, to start this trek without sustenance is insanity! It is crazy to even contemplate you attempted summit of Meru!"

"I appreciate your concern, Tenga, but I assure you, we are full of prana/God's energy—we are oozing with it!"

In the Shadow of a Master

Dr. Robert J. Newton

What was about to transpire would stun Tenga, his Sherpas and others remaining at the base camp. Yeshua told me, "James, watch the prana going down to your feet and lifting you off the ground. I will do the same—let's see what happens!"

Yeshua lifted off the ground and moved forward, levitating. I bravely followed in his wake, in the same manner and I will never really know if I was doing the levitation myself or under the energy of Yeshua but will always know it was a damn cool experience...liberating really!

Meanwhile, Tenga and his Sherpas and the others at camp, thought their eyes were betraying them. I am sure they had to question whether they were hallucinating and might want to cut back on their Cannabis usage. In the distance they could be heard, mumbling among themselves, trying to take in and process what they were witnessing. I'm also satisfied they likened it to something defying the laws of physics and I thought, *like the laws of physics ever impeded Yeshua!*

At first, we moved at the pace of a slow jog and then began to move at the pace of an amazingly fast run. Near the top of Mt Meru, there was a penumbra...a mushroom cloud...causing our ascent to the summit of Everest to be obscured to the people at the base camps.

We could hear the Sherpas proclaim what a fool's errand we were on, and. Tenga, in defense of our actions, refuting that, saying "I would never bet against Master Yeshua!"

While the drama carried out below, Yeshua and I reached a spot just above the penumbra at the summit. We were filled with awe as we silently took in a breath-taking vista, which spread out before us over several hundred miles. The panorama was so striking and momentarily overtook us. Thus, I fully understood the frankness with which Yeshua commented, "Witness the glory of the Lord!"

"Yes, it is humbling yet enthralling, Master," I replied. It is the diametric opposite of the desert we live in!"

After some time and adjusted to having been fully enveloped in the stunning spectacle of snow-covered tall peaks, we started our descent of the mountain, levitating our way downward to Base Camp. The fears of our demise were assuaged once we emerged and were in view below the penumbra, levitating down the slope. With no real cognizance of time, it seemed we had arrived rather quickly, and grateful for the greeting and the meal of jerky and dried fruit. Although neither Yeshua nor I partook of the jerky, we graciously thanked Tenga for the offering of food, acknowledging that Master Yeshua had a benevolence for all life forms, and opposed the killing of livestock and fowl, for sustenance.

Master Yeshua, manifested money from the ethers, and paid Tenga and his Sherpas, thanked them for their help and dismissed them from their service. I am still not sure whether I was surprised or in a state of knowing as Yeshua proclaimed, "James and I will be living up here for a long time to come. We leave you in peace! Namaste...Namaskar!"

In the Shadow of a Master

Dr. Robert J. Newton

CHAPTER 11

IN THE AFTERGLOW OF SUMMITTING MT. MERU, WHAT COULD WE LEARN BY LIVING IN AN ICE CAVE OR AFTER LEAVING, THEREFROM?

YESHUA DID NOT ASK me if I wanted to live in a snow cave but he could read people's thoughts as easy as listening to them speak. To be honest, I had little idea of how this would benefit me or Yeshua, yet since he was always at one with God and in no other state since the day I met him, I had an inherent trust of his decisions and intent.

Living in an ice cave, at a lower elevation, would prove to be marginal at best, for literally all humans. Add to that dynamic...at 18,000, with the atmosphere containing so little oxygen, I knew I was facing a daunting task. I also knew to trust it would not be so for Yeshua, since he had already attained the state of Soruba Samadhi—a completely immortalized body—but I held serious concern that it might well be impossible for me to live there without perishing. Trying to calm myself, I focused on the fact that I had attained a state of intermittent Samadhi, I could well be in a state of quasi samadhi, where my breathing would cease for half an hour, an hour, two hours... up to four hours at a time. So, I was confident that without breathing and utilizing the prana/God energy, life would be circulated throughout my body without the transportation mechanism of my blood.

I knew that to survive, I was literally forced into this intermittent samadhi and to remember always Yeshua's continual message that, "One with God can do anything and everything, regardless of the circumstances, because when we are one with God, we are a majority, connected to our omnipotent God."

And so, I was, and so I did.

We spent hours each day meditating, but took a long hike every day, as well. We did not eat or need food, since our sustenance came from prana/God, as opposed to calories. Yeshua explained this as, "We are in a state of oxidative phosphorylation, James, remarkably similar to how trees and plants sustain themselves. This involves Sun and/or prana, interacting with water, carbon, and magnesium, just like the trees—except they use iron in place of magnesium.

My fear about whether I could survive the harsh elements and thin atmosphere, turned to a state of liberation, as I was no longer tied to the beck and call of hunger., which Yeshua had already been practicing it with great frequency, even before our ice cave hermitage in the snow. Anyway, we were remained in this location for so long, I lost track of actual time and I was sure Yeshua never cared about it anyway. Maybe we could have measured time by the length of our straggly beards for it seemed like we had remained for at least several years, but then...I am just guessing.

In the Shadow of a Master

Dr. Robert J. Newton

One day, Yeshua stood up and stated, "Well, James, God is telling me it is time for us to descend the mountain and re-immerse ourselves in civilization. Before I had time to respond, I found myself in a levitated state of teleportation, and moving swiftly down the mountain, back to the headwaters of the Ganges and then to Badrinath.

We stopped at the Vishnu Hindu Temple and visited with Brahmin Arjun, where Yeshua surprised him when he opened a discussion about sexuality, asking, "Both James and I are old enough to have wives, yet we have none and have never been with a woman. Satguru Agastyar mentioned there is a text about sex, in the Indian tradition, called the *Kama Sutra*. Do you know anything about that?"

"Yes, I do, Master Yeshua, and being married and with progeny, I have not only theoretical knowledge about this, but the experiential aspects of this as well," Arjun replied in an assured and confident manner. "So, Kama Deva/Kama, is the Indian God of Love, and wrote the *Kama Sutra*. He has one wife, Rati, who embodies eroticism, sensuality, and passionate sex. She is very erotic and passionate and raises the sexual desires of Kama to a feverish pitch. After a time of intense, erotic sex, Kama becomes filled with love, and is more attracted to his other wife, Periti, who is more even keeled and more interested in love than sex. That does not mean Kama does not have sex any longer...just, well, that he is more focused on love than erotic sex."

"Now, as you read the Kama Sutra, you will see a miracle of sorts revealed, where there are techniques that temper erotic sexuality by infusing more aspects of love." Arjun continued with a quality of authority that showed in his voice...saying, "This is achieved by slowing down the wild passion of erotic sex...spending more time in foreplay—things like caressing, hugging, kissing, and delaying all penis penetration for as long as possible, or as some experience when engaging in oral sex. This can also be achieved through mudras...positions like the placement of the tongue in the mouth, or keeping the mouth closed as much as possible, and bandam locks, where the anal sphincter muscles are squeezed together many times and for a long time. Actions of this nature prevent and slow the kundalini prana from escaping from the root chakra (tailbone) of the man, very quickly, which allows for more love to be cultivated in the woman and shared to her mate.

If and when the kundalini is released by the man, it will be unleashed with an intensity beyond anything released in an erotic orgasm, focused on orgasm alone—as it bathes the entire body and soul in the kundalini prana...the nectar of God! Sometimes, the man will attempt to prevent the release of his semen, to achieve this, through a bandam lock, but I have found releasing the semen will intensify the orgasm even more, leading to transcendent and altered states of consciousness and love, rarely achievable in other ways, except in Samadhi!"

"Some believe that Kama teaches it is impossible to experience love without pain," Arjun continued with a wry smile on his face. "I believe and actually know that the Love of God is painless, so the pain in love would be intertwined only in passion and eroticism. It is this which the Kama Sutra helps us to circumvent and pull ourselves into *divine love*."

"Amazing," Yeshua replied. "What you just revealed, Arjun, I saw in a vision and I am blessed to have your confirmation of it. How beautiful is this higher aspect of sex, more fully infused with love!"

In the Shadow of a Master

Dr. Robert J. Newton

I could tell Master Yeshua was intrigued what had just confirmed his vision—and rather fascinated to find him never arrogant about something of this nature...or honestly, any other thing! Sitting in quiet repose, I wondered, *how is Yeshua going to use this new knowledge, or how will I, as well?*

In the Shadow of a Master

Dr. Robert J. Newton

CHAPTER 12

MORE PURIFICATION FOR THE IMPENDING MISSION AND MINISTRY OF YESHUA AND HIS FORTUITOUS RETURN TO BETHLEHEM.

YESHUA BEGAN TO SHARE with me what he foresaw in his future. Personally, I sensed he was the Messiah for whom the Jews were looking, and for that matter, the Indians, as well. At the same time, I had an immense trepidation the Rabbi's and Pharisee's would ever accept it, being intransigent in a narrow doctrine. They had walled themselves off, which of course did not provide space for humans as the divine, perfect beings we are!

So different from his normal voice of confidence, I was quite surprised by Yeshua's plaintive intonation as he next stated, "James, I am acutely aware that you and I have the mission to liberate our fellow Jews from the debased status that has been assigned us by the Rabbi's. We learned a lot from the Essenes, where we studied a grander picture and potential for mankind, as per the 7th Name of

God, Aleph Kaf Aleph, which reveals the opposite of what is taught in the synagogues—our inherent perfection—and not that of sinners, as in the sense of bad and evil people, cursed by the acts of Adam and Eve. Remember how the Essenes taught us sin was nothing more than ignorance...not knowing better, and we could never be cursed for the acts of our forefathers?"

What followed next in the conversation was stated with Yeshua with raw sincerity. "James, you must know You have been instrumental in my evolution and an invaluable disciple for me and I am so blessed to have you in my presence. I know I will be having a woman disciple who will become my consort...please do not be jealous of her, as she will complete me—round me out with her feminine love. That is the good news...yet even better news is that she has an alluring friend, of great beauty and love, who will become your consort! In the meantime, James, we must purify ourselves even more, by fasting and praying without ceasing, as we find in 1 Thessalonians 5:17, Daniel 6:10, and Ephesians 6:18."

"The easiest and most effective way to do this, Yeshua continued, "is through the Sanskrit mantras we have learned and your own Hebrew tradition, Kadoish, Kadoish, Kadoish, Adonai, Tsebayoth, as found in Isiah 6:1-3—*Holy, holy, holy, be the Lord God Yahweh, of Hosts.* So, James, what do you say to a bit of light travel to Kashmir to begin our journey through the mountains above Pahalgram, next to the river...with our loyal donkey in tow?"

We thanked Brahmin Arjun for his hospitality and instruction in spiritual sexuality, and as Yeshua began moving us just beyond the speed of light, Arjun watched us vanish into the glowing field of light.

In the Shadow of a Master

Dr. Robert J. Newton

If I had thought our pilgrimage on Meru was the most intense experience possible to endure, I soon was to discover Yeshua found a way to top that! It was not an act of meanness—rather one to prepare us mentally for the arduous ministry ahead, which Yeshua revealed to me as he said, "The best way, James, to prepare for an arduous job is to first endure physical and mental hardships."

So once again we busied ourselves making a home in the snow and ice above Pahalgram, doing Pranayam(a) and Sanskrit mantras like Gayatri and Mahamrityunjaya and the Kadoish mantra. These practices took me into an intermittent Samadhi, whereas Yeshua was already in a continual Soruba Samadhi, wherein he transcended the ravages of the flesh. Again, I lost track of time just as I had on Mt. Meru, yet I could feel my self being cleansed even more...my vibration was being raised, and I came to realize, *it is for me we are doing this—not for Yeshua, because he is already much beyond me in these matters... beyond the beyond!*

A few days later, out of the blue, Yeshua mentioned to me, "James, your light quotient is increasing, day by day. Remember, the linguistic arithmetic of Gematria gives us an equivalency...a co-valence between the Sun and love—and hence between light and Love, because the Sun makes a lot of light?"

I remembered the concept but remained curious as to what he really wanted to convey, so I just shook my head in affirmation and waited for his next comment. "After several years residing here, James, we are now ready to leave the wilderness and go to Sumer [Iran] to see Thoth again. He is known as a great spiritual leader there, as well as in Egypt. So, are you up for another light travel gig, with our fearless donkey in tow? I wonder, shall we call him Hosanna? "

In the Shadow of a Master

Dr. Robert J. Newton

It was clear Yeshua had Mastered light travel like Satguru Agastyar and Satguru Boganathar. We had already undertaken it so many times, the disorientation one experiences moving rapidly through time was no longer even noticeable. There we met with Master Thoth, at the convergence of the Tigris and Euphrates Rivers, at the delta thereof. I was not the least surprised when Thoth remarked, "Yeshua, you are more than ready for your mission— your ministry. And as for you James, I've noticed you are much brighter than when I last saw you."

We both thanked Thoth profusely and bowed before his presence. He responded in kind and as he looked over at us, I could sense he wanted to give a few parting words, since we were making a quick stopover—or so we thought! And then these comments came as he said, "Yeshua, you must be aware—at some level you are—there will be those who betray you when you need them the most, yet James will always hang with you and so will the woman you are about to meet. They will both cleave to you. I would also like you to view this old Sumerian cave with a wheel within a wheel, as is described and revealed in Ezekiel 1:4-16. It created a worm hole—time portal—that many people used to come to Earth from the distant Land of Seth. You, James, and I all came to Earth in this manner. Would you like to see that...go to the cave -so to speak?"

Excited at the prospect of seeing this in person Yeshua replied. "Yes, I would certainly would, Thoth,"

When we subsequently arrived at the time portal, Yeshua exclaimed, "This is most amazing, having these passages in Ezekiel come to life, rather than just reading about it. It appears this is still being used, right, Master Thoth.

In the Shadow of a Master

Dr. Robert J. Newton

Thoth nodded his head up and down, with a smile on his face…a smile that brightly shined in his eyes.

"James and I will use this to go home to Bethlehem…I'm afraid we are growing homesick after close to two decades on our sojourn," Yeshua gratefully replied, "and we do not want to forget our donkey, Hosanna!"

"Enter the middle of the wheel and I will activate the stargate, and send you to your terrestrial home location, my friends," Thoth directed.

We entered the stargate, we were back in Bethlehem, directly, and truly glad to be so. Upon our return, Yeshua and I went to the market, where he was immediately smitten with a young woman— of light and love—who had the glow of the Sun around her. Yeshua, quickly introduced himself to her, saying, "I've not seen anything like you in many years, although I saw exactly you in a vision, some years ago. You must know…James and I have toured much of the world, but if I had known aforehand that you were here, I might never have left"

I didn't want to invade his private conversation, but was too fascinated to do differently, and smiled as he said, "The light streams around you. We must break bread at the café of your choice. What is your name, angelic one?"

"Thank you! My name is Mary Magdala/Magdalene. Please follow me," she said as she stretched out her arm and hand to him. "Follow me please, Messiah!"

Surprise filtered across Yeshua's face as he followed Mary, and he queried, "What makes you think I am a Messiah?"

In the Shadow of a Master

Dr. Robert J. Newton

Mary just smiled at Yeshua, and showing her joy, laughingly replied, "I never waste my time thinking but rather knowing—and know I do! You are, I am confident, a Messiah of our people, because I, too, had a vision about you!"

"Oh, Jesus replied, "you are a prophet/seer, too. This is between you and me and James since using that Messiah moniker will cause me a whole mountain of grief if I proclaim such! You see, people should come to know me from my works, and they already do in much of the world, but just not here—yet! In India, they already call me St. Issa Misiya"

"Hmmm, as you wish, my Master," Mary replied in humble acquiescence. "I know your correct assignation! Let us break bread at this restaurant—they have the best flat bread in Bethlehem and a humus soup with vegetables that will make you want more."

"I will gladly defer to you, Mary," Yeshua responded, completely captivated by Mary's beauty and wiles. Would you consider getting to know each other better? Meeting you makes coming back here from my distant travels begin to make sense."

I could tell by the softness of Mary's face that she was over-joyed at her good fortune. I clearly remembered the conversation where Yeshua and I were told we would meet special women and considered that what might otherwise have looked like a chance meeting may well have been pre-ordained, before they incarnated to Earth. I could see how giddy Mary was when she looked at Yeshua and as I glanced his way, it was obvious he was taken with her, by the way he looked at her!

They started eating before sundown and waned the hours away in each other's company into the wee hours of the night, mostly with Yeshua sharing our varied and vivid travels with Mary.

In the Shadow of a Master

Dr. Robert J. Newton

Needless to say, Yeshua and Mary spent more time conversing, rather than eating the savory food. I could see Brahmin Arjun was right…Yeshua and Mary were a match made in heaven.

As the night drew to an end, Yeshua and I realized we should go home to our parents and let them know their long, lost sons had returned. Yeshua's return was indeed a happy surprise for his parents, but after their happy embraces, Joseph had an equal revelation for his son, proclaiming, "Rejoice, my son, we have found you a beautiful wife…with a nice dowry!"

Yeshua replied in a respectful and grateful manner, saying, "That is great, Father, except for one thing—I found my wife as soon as I got to Bethlehem this afternoon. I had seen her in a vision one night during my travels, thus I knew our paths were destined. We spent the afternoon in a restaurant, talking and eating late into the night."

Being blindsided by his announcement, his mother, Mary, blurted out in a manner foreign for her, "That is quite unconventional, Yeshua!"

"Yes Mother," Yeshua replied, "I understand your response, but when was I ever conventional?"

Stunned to silence, Joseph and Mary just nodded their heads, up and down, not unlike the motion to which I had grown accustomed from Yeshua. I could see they were unhappy, but they intuitively knew to show their begrudging acceptance, through the up and down nodding of their heads,

I elected not to awaken my parents. Thus, morning came and my parents, who arose early, were surprised by my presence. I had been away so long they both had begun to wonder if I was ever going to return. My mother hugged me, and my father did too, shaking my hand first. I gave them an abridged version of my travels with Yeshua and they could tell I was a vastly different person than they knew when I left on my sojourn. I told them about learning the Djed meditation with Thoth, and how Yeshua had a rare meeting with the Oracle of Delphi, meeting and learning from Buddhist monks in Tibet and Nepal, and the many Brahmin priests and Hindu temples we visited, and the yogis we met.

They were spell bound by my stories, but when I told them about ascending the gigantic Mt. Meru and how we had levitated to the top, they were in disbelief, shaking their heads, no! That air of disbelief was compounded when I told them of our several year encampments on the side of Mt. Meru, and our doing the same in an ice cave in Kashmir.

As Yeshua engaged in much the same storytelling at his home, he found his parents were equally aghast. Yeshua felt obligated to give them the details; in reality, he was more concerned about connecting to the soft hand of Mary Magdala/Magdalene. Just before the midday meal, Yeshua rendezvoused with her at the restaurant they had left just hours previously. When Mary Magdala saw Yeshua, she hugged him roundly in a state of unbridled joy.

Yeshua, also in a state of supreme bliss, mentioned how much he missed her, over the rather short night and early morning, as he took her hand and kissed it. He wasted no time mincing words, telling her he wanted her as his wife and how she would need him as his disciple. Yeshua was insistent that their marriage needed to be a private ceremony with only their close families and me. In manner uncustomary for her, Mary gushed her assent to the marriage and it conditions—making it obvious she cared for nothing other than his hand in marriage. She found a well and drew some water...then she washed Yeshua's feet, and subsequently anointed them with olive oil and frankincense. Yeshua commented, "That was not necessary, my beloved wife to be."

Mary responded in kind, "I did such to honor thee...our Messiah! I am a sinner!"

Yeshua responded directly, "I see no sin within you— maybe not understanding your true divinity—possibly ignorant of such, but certainly no transgressional acts against God, me, or anyone else. I sense your heart is pure...that is what attracted me to you, besides your ravishing beauty! I only pray I am worthy of having your as my wife...what an unbridled beauty you are."

That was one of the many Godly qualities possessed by Yeshua, although he was a designated Messiah and head and shoulders above the rest of us, he was humble and unassuming...throughout many years of walking in his shadow, I had never seen him act otherwise!

This momentous occasion was to happen at a time when Yeshua was closing in on his thirtieth year—whilst, his peers had long ago married at about thirteen years of age, after their bar mitzvahs.

In her state of bliss with her union with Yeshua, Mary mentioned to him, "I have a close friend, Mary Salome, who saw your friend, James, and fell hard for him on first sight. Maybe they are soulmates, like you and I, having known each other in other lifetimes. You mentioned to me at our dinner last night, 'Before Abraham was, I AM.' At worst, I could have known you then, right Yeshua?"

In the Shadow of a Master

Dr. Robert J. Newton

"Right you would be, Mary, my love," Yeshua replied resoundingly.

Mary just beamed, as she smiled and laughed about the fortune with her reunion with Yeshua. That day, Mary Magdala/Magdalene sought out Mary Salome. I was in a grand state of mind, being out and about with Mary and our Master, Yeshua. We walked about Bethlehem and to my fortune, we found Mary Salome. To express that I was overjoyed is an understatement; I instantly found her as beautiful and pure as Magdala, and I could tell she had taken a hard liking to me! I thought back to the conversation where Masher Yeshua and I were foretold of these relationships.

I was not surprised when Master Yeshua suggested we go to the town square and discuss our wide-ranging travels and experiences with both Mary's. The idea inspired me, knowing we would share with them stories about us, which would last a lifetime. Although, in part because of our travels, neither Yeshua nor I had the fortune to experience dating or talking to mature women. Thankfully, the events that followed insured we progressed easily and naturally; inexperience most certainly did not handicap us. Oh, how very blessed we were!

CHAPTER 13

THE UNION OF YESHUA AND MARY MAGDALA, ANOTHER POSSIBLE UNION, AND THE BEGINNING OF THE MINISTRY OF YESHUA.

THE UNION OF YESHUA and Mary Magdala (Magdalene) was scheduled to happen in a weeks' time. Courtships in Israel usually did not last long at all, but virtually all unions between and man and a woman were planned out and arranged many years beforehand, so the families intimately knew each other.

This specific marriage would have made news far beyond Bethlehem, if it were not such a private wedding, which, again, was not the norm. Yeshua suggested I ask for Mary Salome's hand in marriage, which stunned me because I had only known her for a day, yet there was no doubt I adored her and would into the foreseeable future. She was like a rare, precious lustrous gem of an exceedingly rare variety. Then, in a way unknown for our time,

In the Shadow of a Master

Dr. Robert J. Newton

Mary Salome said to me, "Is there something you want to tell me because if you do not speak first, I will!"

"Well, Mary (Salome) I do not know if I am worthy of you and it is so early in the game, but would you agree to be my wife? I know I love you and I know you like me, but I can conjecture rather that you, too, love me!"

"Didn't Mary Magdala tell how infatuated with you, I was," Mary (Salome) asked? "I am ready to marry and you're are the one I am ready for, James! Mary Magdala told me about the tantric sex practices you learned from Brahmin Arjun, and that is how I always dreamed my man would treat me, with love and as an equal, which is not currently accepted in our culture!"

I set out to find Yeshua, he held, of course, a far superior understanding than myself about the concept of and the specifics of tantric sex. I found him with Mary Magdala, and with confidence, asked him to explain the theory to my bride to be. I sensed he was incredibly open to doing so because it gave him a chance to explain this to his fiancé, as well. I must confess to being as interested in Yeshua sharing his wisdom with his usual aplomb and confidence.

Quietly, the three of us listened intently as Yeshua explained the story of Lord Kama's two wives, which had been revealed to us by Brahmin Arjun, and how one of them was very erotic, sensual, and intense sexually, yet devoid of love. The other wife was devoted to pure love, and yet when he combined the properties of both wives, he would come to understand what created not only an intense love, but a deep and lasting *divine love supreme*. Both Marys' were overcome with joy and anticipation of their wedding night, knowing the divine blessing and gift they would soon be experiencing!

In the Shadow of a Master

Dr. Robert J. Newton

Both of our fiancée's drew their arms around our necks, so overcome they were with joy and bliss. Fortunately, no one saw their behavior, for in this culture both would have been excoriated for showing affection to a man before they were married. Neither Yeshua nor I complained about it! We both knew we were blessed to have women who would always stand by us!

Yeshua and Mary Magdala suggested we merge our private ceremony of marriage with theirs and be married by a Rabbi in the Temple of Bethlehem, to the exclusion of all other than our private families. During our conversations, as couples we all committed to live far out in the desert in Bethlehem, to avoid attention to ourselves. We deemed this action would not only best benefit us but would serve to not make the town folk uncomfortable with the amount of affection our marriages would display.

Yeshua and I made sure our future wives knew they would be barren, which was unheard of in our time and land...so as to assure we would all attain the highest Dimension of Heaven, which is what God required of women. We taught them of the withholding of semen during sex, knowing it would guarantee their right to the highest Heavenly abode! This sat well with both brides-in-waiting, although both Yeshua and I had significant trepidation, because the practice was completely against our customs of marriage.

Master Yeshua then dropped a bomb on all of us as he boldly and confidently proclaimed, "The key to life and our progression along its path, is to be content and happy, yet never so satisfied as give up on the constant search to improve ourselves." I stopped to consider, *this is exactly how the Creator/God approaches things, constant improvement... constant refinement!*

121

In the Shadow of a Master

Dr. Robert J. Newton

With deep gratitude, I approached Yeshua and gave him a hearty hug. I thanked him, saying, "Master, you never stop amazing me and pushing me to greater heights!" Recognizing my sincerity, I was even more grateful when Yeshua hugged me in return and nodded his head in assent, in that usual, humble manner I come to rely on.

The wedding day was fast approaching for Yeshua and I and we both felt little to no trepidation about the impending event. In fact, anticipation and joy filled our hearts with what was to occur. Our wedding ceremony was truncated to insure we could get in and out of the temple quickly, and not to be scrutinized nor noticed. We managed to do so by entering the temple from the back entrance and leaving the same way. We quickly left for our simple abodes in the remote desert—each couple—hand in hand.

At night, when we consummated our marriages, we used the tantric sexual techniques of Lord Kama, in which we had be instructed by Brahmin Arjun. I never imagined a pure man and a pure woman, like my Mary (Salome,) could inspire the continuing waves of sexual bliss, long after we had experienced our orgasms. Like Arjun instructed, we would experience more than an orgasm...it became an affair of many waves of kundalini energy bliss. One can readily learn about these concepts, but until they experience it, that falls woefully short of useful, as I found when my Mary expressed such a tender love for me—I was sure I was already in the highest realm of the Heavens.

Late the next morning I asked Master Yeshua about what I had experienced, and he shared that even this late in the day he was still experiencing waves of Kundalini energy—long after his initial union with Mary Magdala the night before. He assured me, that from what he had learned, the receptive energy of our wives would make us more complete...and better men and teachers. I could not disagree with him—I was in a position only to shake my head up and down in agreement.

Never one to relax much, Yeshua then mentioned to me, "In a few days, we will begin our ministry to the masses. They are hungry for more than just reading the Torah. After a while, it becomes bland and boring, like it was for you and me, James."

"I am willing, ready, and able to start when you need me, Master," I exclaimed with a firm voice that spoke of my certitude." I know Mary Salome will be there to aid us, as well as your venerated wife, Mary Magdala. I have come to realize and graciously accept that she will take my place as your right-hand man—supplanting me, although she be a woman. I understand my place and your example, Yeshua. Let me express how often your humble, egoless approach has taught me to be the same, or at least close, thereto." My comment was followed by a singular thought, *I hope.*

In the days that followed, we went out and began to spread the higher teachings of God, where we found men who already wanted to help Yeshua spread his gospel. There were others whom Yeshua quickly recruited because he sensed they were filled with the spirit of the Lord. Many of these men were fisherman or farmers...common people who were not from the rabbinical class...the clergy.

Yeshua found this not to be a problem. Rather, it was beneficial, for he did not have to struggle to re-educate them—or convince them of a new way to view humanity and God, far beyond the limited precepts of the Rabbi's. Jesus took a disciple, John, who Jesus chose for a time as his head disciple—elevated beyond either me or

In the Shadow of a Master

Dr. Robert J. Newton

Mary Magdala. Jesus had John baptize him, by submersing his head in water, to purify him, in the River Jordan, near Bethany. John did not feel worthy to baptize Jesus, because he knew Jesus would baptize people with the Holy Spirit and with fire, something Jesus learned in India: how to use Yagna/fire, to perform a higher purification than from water.

After being baptized by John, Yeshua went into the desert alone and fasted and meditated, as he had done for years in India and Kashmir. Upon the completion of a retreat of many days, Yeshua summoned me, my wife, Mary Salome, his beloved wife, Mary Magdala, and a few other Disciples, including John, to Galilee. It was at the sea there where Yeshua began to teach; to preach.

At first, the congregants were small in number, but as I plied my way about Galilee, spreading the presence and word of Yeshua, people started to throng to see him. They came to hear his message of the divinity of all men and women, and how to turn away from sin, which he specifically equated to being ignorant...simply not knowing better. The Master exhorted the masses to surrender to God and become the divine people—which they came to know was their divine inheritance and right to claim! One Rabbi, under the guise of a common person, went to hear Yeshua and tried to quarrel with him in an overt attempt to discredit him. The masses, however, were enthralled with what Yeshua was teaching them, singled out the Rabbi, and rousted him from the crowd.

Unfortunately,, this did not end the trouble the Rabbi would create, as he told the Pharisees about Yeshua's heretical doctrine, to stir up further opposition to my Master. At some level, I understood their perspective. After all, their job was to protect the integrity of the Torah. Watching the conflict build before me, I thought, *from*

124

In the Shadow of a Master

Dr. Robert J. Newton

Yeshua's perspective, his teaching and the Jewish scriptures are not mutually exclusive—they cross clarify each other.

There were many opportunities to observe Yeshua manifest fish and bread and water from which his congregants partook. Sometimes...he manifested that sustenance literally from the ethers and at other times... by taking small amounts of food and multiplying such, vastly. More than once, such as at a wedding in Cana, Yeshua turned water into wine. Yeshua's myriad events were not limited to a particular geographic area; they happened at the Sea of Galilee and Decapolis—the group of ten cities on the eastern frontier of the Roman Empire, which had formed collectively because of their language, culture, location, and political status, were dependent on Rome; they occurred at what came to be known as *the Sermon on the Mount,* where Jesus first shared his beatitudes, which was on a mountain near the Lake of Gennesaret and Capernaum, the fishing town on the northern shore of the Lake of Gennesaret.

When the Rabbis and Pharisees heard about his engagement with and influence over so many, they became envious and were spurred to attack the Master, even more. More than once, Yeshua was seen walking on water, once crossing the Sea of Galilee, to the city of Gesara. Others were in quite a state of awe; however, it surprised me not at all since we had both levitated to the top of Mt. Meru.

Again, and again...the criticism of Yeshua reared its ugly head; he was called a practitioner of black magic and determined to be possessed by evil in order to perform these feats. The irony of this disparagement was that Jesus overcame the temptation of evil, often. One event in particular sticks out in my mind. Yeshua was in the Judean Desert, where he was being constantly tempted by the forces of evil to no avail—because his connection to the light of God, as in the 59th Name of God, in Exodus of the Torah, Hey Resh Chet. The Master, by now, knew resolutely there was no benefit for him to separate himself from the light and fire—with its continual and constant guidance derived from God.

Yeshua also raised people from the dead, including Lazarus. This was never meant as a means to glorify himself, but rather his father which was in Heaven! Following this particular healing, he was once again accused of being possessed by the devil, to be able to do such. I rather felt Yeshua was on a roll as his miracles continued to occur. The political repercussions however, caused, Mary Magdala, Mary Salome, and me no small measure of anguish. I mentioned our concerns to Yeshua, and his response was quick and to the point, as he exclaimed, "You have been a warrior in many of your previous incarnations and a staunch defender of truth, James, and that is what makes you want to protect me from the insults of the rabbis and pharisees. But please temper your emotions! Don't misunderstand. It isn't that I don't appreciate your defense of me, but my purpose—and yours, too—is to win our critics over with love...God's irresistible love!"

On one occasion, Yeshua took his consort (Mary Magdala), James, John, and Peter (his closest Disciples), and me to Mt. Herma, where a transfiguration occurred. We gathered round watching while his true body was revealed as only Spirit/energy—most radiantly so. He later spoke with me of his experience—wherein he was transfigured before us, asking, "James, did my face really shine as the sun, and my raiment turn as white as the light?"

In the Shadow of a Master

Dr. Robert J. Newton

I confirmed we had shared that experience; I also assured him that Moses and Elijah were there conversing with him.

My memory also serves me well as I recall seeing Yeshua at the Sea of Galilee when he asked the throng to let the children in the crowd come forward. I clearly remember thinking, *this is Yeshua's lesson to subtly teach the masses, through showing the example and the innocence of children...and their endless curiosity...and their divinity, still not besmirched by false human beliefs!*

Many people, hungry for an inspiration that was sadly lacking in the sermons of the rabbis in the synagogues, thirsted after his messages. Some said he was doing little more than feeding his ego in preaching to the masses. I knew that not to be so! I had walked in his shadow for over two decades and always, always...found him to be the most humble and unassuming man who had ever walked the face of the Earth—certainly, at least in my lifetime.

Many times I saw Yeshua, so infused with light and love, his head and body shone as an intense sunlight, like at the transfiguration at Mt. Herma—it was this light, which caused the multitudes that came to the Sea of Galilee to move forward and crowd around him. On one of our walks, Yeshua shared one of his concerns with me, "James, although I am glad I am able to spread a message of love and bring hope and salvation to mankind, I am decidedly more interested in conveying the greater message of the supreme divinity of woman and man, which I trust I have often shared with you.

The Master was fanatical that people understood his miracles could be performed by them. He repeated many times how they could perform even greater works than those performed by him. However, other than James, Mary Magdala/Magdalene, and Mary

127

In the Shadow of a Master

Dr. Robert J. Newton

Salome, none of the other Disciples or congregants seemed to be able to grasp this critical concept!

When Yeshua realized he was about to be arrested, he had two Disciples find a suitable place in Jerusalem, for a Passover Supper, where they would all break fasting. There was a lot of consternation among Yeshua's Disciples about what they would do and how they would function without their Master and Messiah/Wayshower. Many of the Disciples came to what had become accepted as Yeshua's head disciple, Mary Magdala/Magdalene. Over time they had come to place Mary above other male disciples in knowledge and influence and asked her to address their Master about their concerns and questions.

The Disciples looking to Mary caused a great amount of jealousy in John, who was the previous head disciple, and further, did not even remotely consider any woman to be his equal. What he did not realize is that I was the head disciple at one time, and Yeshua subsequently asked me to step down because John was better known among his followers than me.

Sadly, neither did John understand the importance of the Sophia Christ...the feminine Christ...which was exemplified by Mary Magdala/Magdalene and completed Yeshua, like no other could! She remained in the background but that never diminished her importance or the necessity for Yeshua to have her to complete him.

Mary answered the Disciples, saying, "Yeshua will be betrayed by one of his Disciples but his indictment will come from the insistence of the Pharisees, who despise him! Do not be long concerned because he, a son of God, and cannot be defiled. I also remind each of you, as his Disciples, to remember and repeat his

128

Lord's Prayer, which is from your Father...which is in Heaven, whose name is hallowed, whose kingdom is done and whose will must be done—on Earth as it is in Heaven."

Stopping a moment to ensure each Disciple was carefully listening to her, Mary continued to deliver Yeshua's message. "Remember, too, that you will be given your daily bread and sustenance, and that as you will be forgiven your debts, you should forgive your debtors." It was important to remind the Disciples of the debt/loan cancellation, known as Jubilee, which kept them from being in a constant state of impoverishment.

She also admonished them, saying, "You should shun temptation, stay clearly focused on God—and only God—and be delivered from evil...for God is the Kingdom and the Power and the Glory forever, for all men and women."

Mary Magdala/Magdalene also urged the Disciples to pray without ceasing, noting that as he had taught them—as he was taught by God. She repeated that a good way to engage in this unceasing prayer, was to repeat the Kadoish Mantra/Prayer, continuously and sequentially, for at least 108 times in one session. She refreshed their memories about this particular chant as she repeated it to them, *Kadoish, Kadoish, Kadoish, Adonai, Tsebayoth (Sephiroth)*, and further reminded them that this praise to the LORD GOD OF HOSTS would never leave them short or abandoned.

Following supper Yeshua reminded the Disciples that no matter what, he would be back. The indictment and trial of Yeshua was believed to be the result of his betrayal by disciple Judas, although in reality, it was at the insistence of the Pharisees, who despised Yeshua for his new better and uplifting teachings. The Pharisees alleged Yeshua claimed he was the Messiah—the Son of

In the Shadow of a Master

Dr. Robert J. Newton

God. When his judge, Pontius Pilate, the currently acting Roman governor asked Yeshua about this assertion, Jesus correctly answered he never claimed to be either. That was consistently typical of him!

Pilate rightfully determined Yeshua had committed no crime—and found no fault in him. Unfortunately, this decree did not assuage the Pharisees; they remained insistent Yeshua should be crucified, to which demands Pilate eventually relented.

I watched as Yeshua's Disciples were drowning in grief, yet based on our journey together, I knew he was not concerned...he had already existed for many years in the immortalized state of Soruba Samadhi into which he had been initiated in India. When the radicals placed a crown of thorns on his head and spikes in his hands, Yeshua did not bleed. It caused quite a commotion among his executioners...his followers...his Disciples. None understood that in the state of Soruba Samadhi Yeshua had no heartbeat and blood did not flow through his veins. In the crowd, I was less discomforted than others; I recognized when Jesus drifted off into a deep state of meditation on the cross and was presumed to be dead—exhibiting no pulse or heartbeat—when in fact he was not!

When he was taken down from the cross, Yeshua appeared dead to everyone and as was the custom, was put in a tomb. Once encased in the burial chamber, one would have found him alive and kicking. I often thought if I were with him there, I'd see him nodding up and down, with a wry smile on his face. Given all I'd learned on our journey, it is highly likely he spent a lot of time, leaving the tomb and moving about the area where he was believed to be interred.

As Mary Magdala later recounted to me, when she came by to check on her husband at his tomb, she was not anguished he was not there; she was only concerned as to his whereabouts. Shortly after she found her husband, I came by with my Mary (Salome), and we rejoiced to see Mary Magdala/Magdalene embracing and kissing our Master. We knew Yeshua could not be killed but neither the other Disciples nor Yeshua's followers could comprehend what had transpired...although he had foretold many times exactly what had transpired. Holding Mary (Salome) in my arm, I thought, *this is just too much of a stretch for them...with their existing belief systems.*

Over the course of the next 40 days, Yeshua met with his Disciples 10 times—after he revealed a body unharmed by the ravages of death. Other than Mary Magdala/Magdalene, Mary (Salome) and me, it remained difficult for them to truly comprehend what happened, On the 40th day following his emergence from the tomb, Yeshua ascended into the Heavens, from the Mt. of Olives. As I watched, I thought, *this is much the same way in which he may have come to Earth—from The Land of Seth, deep on the Milky Way Galaxy.* However, what virtually no one realizes, other than those of us in his very inner circle, is Yeshua—now known as Jesus—has visited us often! He repeatedly told me, "If you call out my name...if you see my face...I will be there for those who need my help. I AM always available to lead those in need to our Father which art in Heaven! I am here to take you to Heaven!

My thoughts were, *how blessed we are to have him and his consort, Mary Magdala/Magdalene, as our conduits to God, and for me walk in his shadow and learn from the Master!*

Shalom! Kadoish, Kadoish, Kadoish, Adonai, Tsebayoth!

131

In the Shadow of a Master

Dr. Robert J. Newton

Note: Mt. Meru was never summited until 2011, in modern times, by three of the best mountain climbers in the world—Conrad Anker, Jimmy Chin, and Renan Ozturk. It took them two expeditions, and on the first one, one of the climbers broke two legs; they ran out of food 300 feet from the summit and had to descend. On the second expedition, one of the climbers became so sick his mates were sure he was going to die. There is a documentary film revealing how excruciatingly hard and dangerous it is to scale this mountain via the Sharks Fin Route they took. They compared Mt. Everest, which they had scaled two times, as no more than a hike.

About the Author

Dr. Robert J. Norton has lived much of his life in the way he writes...flavored by a deeply passionate quest to surround himself with the highest level of knowledge in the myriad areas that ensure we live rich, full lives. His education has been extensive, ranging from Speech and English at Cal State Fullerton, to a Juris Doctorate from American College of Law, and many certifications in alternative healing. He formalized his career in Naturopathic Medicine as a graduate of Clayton School of Natural Healing.

Newton has lived to serve others...operating as an award-winning landscape and design company for many years; as a Christian Science healer to two decades, and more recently...as an author, speaker and life and relationship coach.

Yoga, Metaphysics, Spiritual Sciences, Natural Healing, World Religions, ancient Hermetic teachings—this PHILOSOPHER and

CHAMPION FOR THE WORLD tapped into the roots of spirituality, sexuality, life, and love…all with the purpose to enlighten those with a common desire to utilize multiple methods and strategies to approach life more effectively, creatively, radiantly, and with great abundance.

Today, Dr. Newton lives his life looking forward…honoring the love and the beliefs he shared with his wife, Ann, a vivid character in many of his books—and writing more novels to plant a "what if" seed in the minds of his avid readers.

Dr. Newton continues to provide a series of classes and book signings around North and South America, as he teaches and initiates people into the very practices that lead to immortality.

Please feel free to contact Dr. Newton for more specifics on his various events at:

www.drrobertnewton.com

Theta4ia@yahoo.com

You can also stay connected with him on the following social media platforms.

Amazon Author Central:

https://www.amazon.com/Dr.-Robert-J.-Newton/e/B00LR6A402

Author Website:

http://www.robertjnewtonauthor.com

Professional Website:

www.drrobertnewton.com

Twitter:

https://twitter.com/DrRobertNewton

Goodreads:
https://www.goodreads.com/author/show/18159569.Dr_Robert
_Newton

Facebook:

https://www.facebook.com/robert.newton3

https://www.facebook.com/anAngel.not perceived

In the Shadow of a Master

Dr. Robert J. Newton

More Books by This Author

Follow this prolific writer at Amazon Author` Central (Paperback and Digital Versions)

https://www.amazon.com/default/e/B00LR6A402

1) **A Map to Healing and Your Essential Divinity Through Theta Consciousness**: The Physics of the Immortal "Light Body" and the Creator's Template of Perfection and Abundance for His People (2012)

https://www.amazon.com/Healing-Essential-Divinity-Through-Consciousness-ebook/dp/B0792WXKKT

2) **Pathways to God:** Experiencing the Energies of the Living God in Your Everyday Life (2012)

https://www.amazon.com/Pathways-God-Experiencing-Energies-Everyday-ebook/dp/B0792X14SS

3) **The Hidden Codes of God**: A Journey to the Unknown Secrets and Dimensions of the Divine and the Energy of Love (2015)

https://www.amazon.com/Hidden-Codes-God-Journey-Dimensions-ebook/dp/B00VA0TZ9G

4) Beyond the Mists of Time: When Trees Ruled the Earth and The State of Balance and Euphoria That Ensued There From (2015)

https://www.amazon.com/Beyond-Mists-Time-Balance-Euphoria-ebook/dp/B00VAN8L8Y

5) In Search of the Body Immortal: Let the Journey Begin (2015)

https://www.amazon.com/Search-Body-Immortal-Journey-Begin-ebook/dp/B016LGBUW8

6) Planet of the Stupids: Bringing Back the Light of God to Planet Earth—With a Paradise Found (2016)

https://www.amazon.com/Planet-Stupids-Bringing-Earth-Paradise-ebook/dp/B01DL1MKH0

7) The Immortality Prophecy: Let the Reveal Begin! (2016)

https://www.amazon.com/Immortality-Prophecy-Let-Reveal-Begin-ebook/dp/B01IRS689I

8) A Nation of Deceit: A Nation Deceived ~ A Nation Aggrieved Finding A Solution ~ A New Evolution! (2016)

https://www.amazon.com/ANationofDeceit-ANation Deceived-Aggrieved-Evolution-ebook/dp/B01MG1NBJ

9) In Search of the Hidden Codes of God in the Mathematics of Gematria: Discovering the True Da Vinci Code

https://www.amazon.com/Search-Hidden-Codes-Mathematics-Gematria/dp/0996137165/

10} **An Angel Not Perceived:** Leaving the Realms of Heaven and Descending to Earth   (Jan 22, 2020)

https://www.amazon.com/ANGEL-NOT-PERCEIVED-Leaving-Descending-ebook/dp/B0844P3L7H/

11**)**   **A Nation of Deceit**: Revenge of the Deep State (Oct 20, 2020)

https://www.amazon.com/Nation-Deceit-Revenge-Deep-State-ebook/dp/B08LYYVZ8R

PRINT: https://www.amazon.com/dp/0996137181